ALONE

... But Never Lonely

Katherine

Written by K. Lee

KLE PUBLISHING
www.KLEPub.com

Alone... But Never Lonely: Katherine

Published by Krystal Lee Enterprises (KLE Publishing)

Please send comments and questions:

Krystal Lee Enterprises
1007 Green Street Suite SE #1635 Conyers GA 30012
www.KLEPub.com   770-240-0089

Printed in the United States of America.

ISBN: 978-0-9971378-2-8
Library Control # 2016918197

Book Production: KLE
Cover Design: KLE: Justin Thomas

I pay tribute to my Lord and Savior Yeshua (aka Jesus) the Christ.

A dedication to my girls and I pray that they grow in the fullness of life, benefiting, learning from the profits, experience, the works I create in my life.

Second, may all who read this book find a nugget that helps them maneuver through life; that eases a burden and provides insight to live vicariously through the moments that will be of value in the present or the future.

Special thanks to: My Mom, My Siblings, Grandparents, Nancy, Trinice, Carlos, Anna, Rob, Family (Aunts, Uncles, Cousins), Friends (Facebook & LinkedIn included) and My Teachers for encouraging me through the years as well as the support. I love you all.

Foreword

If you think this book is about a battered woman who broke free and escaped torment, this book is not quite that. This is a story about a woman and her struggles while alone in the mist of traditional life events. Graduating high school, dating, getting married, staying married, and divorce all happen every day. These life experiences or the lack thereof are the stones cast into the water and the follow up decisions is the ripple.

Not every relationship should progress to marriage and it is not a sad day for every marriage to end. This book documents what happens to most of us when we get ahead of ourselves and commit a lifetime to the wrong person for the right reasons. What happens when love dries up or perhaps reality is revealed and the person staring you in the face no longer seems to fit in your puzzle? You both now can't look each other in the face, so it seems no better option then to be alone to work out the details.

Not every marriage created on earth is Godly appointed. In fact, many are done out of fear, impatience, and the desire to experience a wedding ceremony even if the only real thing is the expense. Life is full of twist and turns and no one knows the future. Marriage is our stab at believing in a perfect dream. We attempt to have a perfect marriage or union when imperfect people establish the union—with prayerfully a perfect God at the center. Is there a solution for guaranteed success?

With the best of circumstances many find themselves alone. Alone in the marriage, alone because of divorce, alone because we didn't settle or the other gave up. This series is for those who know they are not crazy. They gave their life, relationship or marriage their best and yet are alone. You can be alone but that doesn't mean you are lonely!

When we, you are alone, it is time to date yourself, discover, and experience life with you! To start a new relationship or expect new life in an established relationship is to strive amiss without a renewed mind. We must learn who we are, be true to ourselves, and fight for what we want and need without settling.

There are deal breakers we all should have and we should not be ashamed of them. If you are unable to stay with your spouse if they cheat on you, and you find they have, you are not a failure if you leave and honor your deal breaker. If you find that forgiveness is in your heart, forgive and be prepared to work like mad to get back whatever was lost. Neither of the two is weak if they are true to themselves.

The strength is in being true to yourself and making choices with your eyes wide open. I trust this book will encourage you to find yourself and remember there is value in being alone…because you are never lonely. Living alone allows the much-needed time for you to spend with you and remember why everyone in your mist must respect you—even if they don't like you today or ever.

Chapters:

Introduction

I have two beautiful children born from two different relationships and I would like to think, two totally different situations. The more I ponder my romantic life the more I can't help but think: "Did I do the relationship thing right?" Is it possible I gave up when I should have pressed on? Am I quitter or a person who understands the difference to ceasing from continuing in error?

Am I just a failure at love that continues to miss the boat? Or perhaps, I keep boarding the wrong boat that sails me in the wrong direction and when I realize it, I jump off. Regret creeps in only when I see love on a TV screen.
Growing up I always valued love, relationships, and marriage. Like many young girls I dreamt about falling in love and marrying the man of my dreams. My grandparents, The Lancaster's and The Fisher's have made me admire love. My two sets of grandparents have been married since I can remember and one until death; may Granddaddy Fisher rest in peace. Seeing my grandmothers cook every day and make awesome Sunday meals; watching my grandfathers entertain our large families, keeping us together, and demonstrating an everlasting love toward my grandmothers—I wanted that.

As I grew older that vision became deem. The idea of marrying an ideal man wasn't a dream but a looming nightmare. I know, wow, sharp contrast. Long story short, my childhood wasn't ideal and the relationships I saw go terrible wrong made me fear men instead of want to embrace them. I had my fair share of dates gone wrong, nowhere, and flat out rejection. I grew to think perhaps I wasn't cut out for marriage. Maybe I made an ideal mistress—but my faith wouldn't allow me to cope with that.

So, I decided, perhaps I was meant to be alone. Meant to wake up with no one near me. Have a house full of dogs—trained dogs. I have never been a cat person—except for when I had a fluffy white Persian cat named Chase. I loved that cat; he acted like a dog and feared nothing. My desire for children growing up became non-existent. Especially because I thought about us living in the last days and the confusion, fear of the rapture being near. I remember telling my mother I didn't want children and wanted to be like my Aunt Von. She never married or had children and unfortunately died young from breast cancer in her 30's. Bless her soul and all people who survived, struggling, and fallen from the big "C."

Being alone is such a scary word to aging women and men concerned that their baby-making clock may have ticked its last tick years back. I am writing this book to share some thoughts I have about relationships, being alone, and a journey that I believe both male and female alike can

identify. The conclusion of this book doesn't promise any yellow brick road to happiness; but shares
a story about lessons learned that may help with
how you view being alone—but know, that doesn't
make you lonely.

Background

The absolute worst question to ask a person that is alone, "So when are you planning on getting married and having some kids?" Growing up the question was similar to asking me, "When are you going to give up your dreams, chase your husband around, and pray to be remembered for anything you do right in your life?" When I was eighteen fresh out of high school, I though I was ready for the world. I was told all my life I was mature for my age, so I was ready. I thought maneuvering through life and staying out of romantic affairs would be a breeze.

I couldn't date in high school, never left the house unless it was college or work related. In high school, I attended a magnet school so I was triple focused on what I wanted to do with my life. I knew I loved production, entrepreneurship, business, law, accounting, acting, dancing, modeling, theater, and speaking.

I also desired to keep my options open for how I could express myself with some newly found hobby. I have to admit, although I didn't date, I did have crushes. I didn't disclose my crushes until I was 18 and almost leaving the house. My first kiss was at 18 and French kiss was 19.
I crushed on Arthur for 2 years before telling him

I liked him. We met at a theme park, a place where many life events will trickle back in this book. I remembered I only told him because a friend and co-worker passed away unexpectedly. Marcus was a great guy, kind, funny and yet quiet. I never knew all the details but learned he died from a car accident.

I realized we don't have until forever. If you have something to say that you don't want to die with, sometimes it is best you just say it. That day took much nerve but I am sure he already knew. We walked to our cars together after work and when I reached my car I told him. His almond eyes, and nice smile, embraced my words and he asked could he kiss me.

My first kiss was sweet, and then I feared if anyone saw. My stepfather at the time was known for stalking. I thank the Lord he didn't know. After that encounter he asked me the next time we worked together if I wanted to hang out.

We took a stroll through the park and ended on the side where the manatees roamed in their tanks. As he joked, smiled, and laughed, girlishly I thought of us being a couple. It just seemed right. As we stood in line waiting to enter the exhibit, he told me he liked me too. We entered into the theater and as the lights dimmed for the presentation, he told me he loved my eyes, my smile, and my laugh. He admired this and that and he was surprised I liked him.
He soon after said he wasn't ready for a relationship because he had recently broken up with his

girlfriend some weeks back; he still loved her. I told him I understood, and now isn't a good time for me; my stepdad wasn't having it. I was moving to go past him and he took me by my hand and kissed me. My first French kiss was there inside the Manatee Exhibit.

Arthur and I danced around dating for a year until I realized he didn't want me. He told me I wasn't experienced and I should know more about myself. After many discussions to prove to him otherwise, I agreed. I can't say I loved him, but I thought I did. It was hard for me to digest how a man could love a woman that was unfaithful and broke up with him; and here I am, patient, waiting, showing up to events, paying others no mind. Yup…I was that one.

Then, one day I just stopped. I moved on and I got experiences. About a year later, he wrote me a letter apologizing for the way things went between us. He acknowledged my efforts but it was too late. I got serious about the Lord, my life's direction, and had already started dating the man I would marry.

In romance I was not a great thinker—perhaps, but for school I was fantastic. I do believe I am a left-brain thinker gone right. You see, in middle school I had a strong love for science and math that in high school flipped to English, writing, and creative expression. I earned a scholarship to attend a 4-year science program at a University in Tennessee while in middle school.

I thought about taking advantage of the

scholarship up until the ending of my eight-grade year. I realized science might not be the best field of study for me because I felt the subject forced people into a box. I like to be free.
In science, theories are stated and then must undergo experimentation to prove them true or false. The test results are then thrown as a blanket over a large population that many cannot be accurately represented; because people, although maybe slight at times, are different and therefore many experiments will only be true to the subjects. So, I figured science and I would bump heads.

My desire to be a psychologist decreased also because of warnings by adult friends. "You don't want to sit at a desk and hear people's problems all day" was the popular warning. I decided perhaps I didn't want to hear one sad story after another, but I do want to help people.

When in college I took a sociology class that I found intriguing but it still wasn't me. I remember thinking you shouldn't stereotype a region based on a small study because you will always find a person contrary to your findings. I am sure generalities do have their place, but I don't want to see people or life that way. I fell in love with writing because good writing is based on telling accounts, situations, and experiences based on life events or true feelings. Great movies and songs are usually based on real joy, pain, hurt, and sorrow.

Loving to write allowed me to tap into every area in my creative and corporate scope that interested me and bring it all together. As a young child I was always an entertainer. Funny, my mom named me after a television host that had a similar name to my mother's sister, Krystal, better known as Aunt Kris. My mom wanted to name me Krystal but my aunt said the name "didn't do much" for her so give me something original.

My mom saw a lady named Kathy on TV and decided to spell my name with a "K." Katherine was close to Krystal and the "K" was the same as my mom's sister; she felt she killed two birds with one stone. As a child we use to play games that I honestly think economic challenges helped us to create. "Make Me Laugh," "Caboose", and "Dance Time" were the games we frequently played and made us all comedians.

Our family would play these games for hours and usually ended because someone got physically hurt while performing a stunt that always got laughs. I remember one of the funniest moments was playing caboose with my uncle. Uncle Travis, would sit on the floor and we would volunteer to be catapulted into the air and discover a creative way to land.

My oldest brother who was always very tall if you ask me, but I am 5'0, full grown, so perhaps not the best person to ask; but nonetheless he mounted our uncle's feet. The four children that were onlookers and our Mom watched shaking our heads because my uncle's knees were into his chest. We knew this caboose was going to be it for the night.

As his legs released and sent the oldest of my

mom's five children soaring through the air, Kevin cleared the entire living room and ended up crashing foot first into the TV stand, breaking the door off and exposing the VHS tapes behind it. We all roared into laughter and through tears we asked him, "Are you okay?" He was alright except his butt stung as it hit the floor with a powerful thud.

I think we all aged so incredibly well because we learned to laugh. There were serious times at my mom's house that was no laughing matter; but I believe many of us learned and kept on laughing to keep from crying. I learned growing up not everything that happens in your life can be understood, but it is what it is so try to make the best of it.

I believe the core of how you perceive the world around you starts with the culture of your home. We were all raised to see each other as family and even though we didn't all share the same father, because we had the same mother we never called each other step anything. To this day, my siblings and I are very close and I thank my mom for instilling that in us.

Bullied? Yes

Another valuable lesson I learned as a child growing up in a large family, teamwork is not an option. We all succeed or failed together. I am not a supporter of violence, but a strong proponent that there is power in words; however, in my mother's home we were raised that if one of us got into a fight we all had to fight.

I have not technically been in a fight in my entire life, as far as a person pushing or punching me and then enticing me to fight them back. I have gotten a rock and a glass bottle thrown at me. I also got slapped in the face twice once by a confused man who had a romantic misunderstanding and the other by my baby sister, Erica, who I slapped back before my mother gave us both a whipping.

The rock was in elementary school. There was a young boy that was in a grade one or two levels higher than me. His twin brothers both liked me, but I wasn't allowed to date in elementary school obviously. So I told the twins what my mom said, and their older brother caught up with me after school. Asked me did I like his brothers? I said "No." He asked did I like him, I said "No."

As he called me names and ran off to catch up with his friends, he stopped and picked up a quarter sized rock and threw it at me. The rock hit me in my right cheek and it stunned me for a second. I couldn't believe what just happened. As I ran for home, tears ran down my face and confusion filled my head. I never pictured violence being evidence for a crush or love. That was an emotional day and my brother and sister got chewed out because they weren't there to help.

Later in life, middle school, there was a boy that followed me after school. I decided to start roller blading home because I was much faster on skates than running. I was never a track star, hated running in my youth in fact. I found out later from his own lips he liked me and asked would I be his girlfriend. Again, my answer was "No." He threw a glass bottle at me that hit the ground and broke as I skated away.

I still enjoy skating although in Tennessee, the sidewalks and streets are not safe because the hills are lethal. I tried it one time and could not stop the wheels from rolling. I was skating around my mom's community and I enjoyed the breeze in the air. As I rolled down the street I realized I eased onto a hill and couldn't stop by spinning.

So I did the next best thing, I jumped on the curb to slow down and if I was going to fall I decided the grass was safer than cement. Something about getting older that makes falling dangerous, scary, or comical. Today if I fall I find it comical but as I get older dangerous and fearful maybe more accurate. I do go to a ring whenever I have the chance to keep my skills somewhat consistent with my youth.

To be fair, I have to tell you, that I didn't always have the best balance even in the best of circumstances. When I was first learning to skate, I was scared to fall; so I decided to roller skate in the house to practice. This was a great idea at the time, but soon my mom would holler from inside of the house, "Stop all that skating on that porch." I didn't listen, I was in a groove, and kept on skating. I didn't register that the porch was full of windows waist high and if I couldn't stop a glass window would be my brake.

So not even five minutes after, I tried to break and couldn't. I went through the window but thank the Lord I didn't fall out. I broke the glass and my mom came out and snatched me back in. I didn't have one cut on my face, arms, hands, and if it wasn't instant terror for my mom, I am sure I would have gotten a whipping.

In high school I got slapped once in the face and the second time in the back of the head but it wasn't by a high school student; to go deeper into that story would require another book. So I go on to say, boys were not my only problem. I had a few females in my life that didn't like me.
In elementary school it was the girl that pushed me into the mud because her kid brother liked me. Later I found out it was deeper than that. Her mother came to the school, fell in love with me and nick named me Kiwi. Her daughter and I be- came good friends because we were forced to get to know each other.

I hung out at their house several times where

I enjoyed eating kiwis, talking to the mother, and playing checkers. This was usually the case with the girls that didn't like me. Once they got to know me, potential enemies became my friends and would later defend me. This was true on through high school, where my best friend Jazz, was willing to fight a girl because she didn't like what the girl said about me.

I remember having to tell her, there is no reason to fight about lies. Anyone that knows me, know I am not a gossip. Anything I had to say about a person I would tell them to their face. Prayerfully, I could be of help and not a tool for humiliation was always the goal. I was picked on as a child and I didn't like it; but constructive criticism I was always on board to listen to.

Needless to say, the girl apologized to Jazz and I, and the three of us clicked and was cool through high school. I was nervous going to high school because of the horrible bully stories my mom told me about in her experience. The worst account my mom could remember was her being chased home by 10 girls who wanted to fight her. She said it was her pretty eyes and personality that drew the boys.

The girls were so adamant about jumping my mother they chased her for over 4 blocks. She ran those blocks screaming for help and not one person came from their house or called the cops. As she got in earshot of her grandmother's house, her grandfather heard her screaming from up the block; he came out with a shotgun. The girl's feet instantly became cemented to the concrete.

They all turned around slowly then darted home. There were no more problems for my mom, as she would say "in the Chi" after that. The "Chi," translated into English means Southside of Chicago. I thank the Lord I didn't have any moments where I could have been jumped and perhaps because I was a bookworm. Every second I was not studying to pass a test with a 90 or better, I was reading a book about Africa, Native American Fiction and Non-fiction, and of course the Harry Potter series.

A series I absolutely loved was "The People of" a Native American series that had people of the earth, moon, thunder, etc. My older sister Vickie and I read every book in the series. I admit my sister was a much faster reader than I. I use to joke I liked to savor every word and she had to be skipping every other word to go that fast. We're both still readers and I am sure she can out-read me today. I know a nerdy game.

Read, Write, Study—Cool

It was a good thing I was a reader because when I reached the 11th grade, I was dual enrolled in college. Taking night courses was a breeze and a great escape from my abnormal reality. I saw education as my ticket out of the mentality of the "hood," to better my life, and to make it. So many people looked up to me and desired my success; I would have felt horrible not to make anything of myself.

I also desired to bring my younger siblings from Alabama back to Georgia. They left to live with their dad when I was in middle school and I missed them terribly. Later I would get my wish and for a season we five were all in Georgia again.

Little did I know that would require for them both to live with me and at one point at the same time. Something happens as siblings get older, it is possible to be too much alike. They function like magnets, they repel when like sides get close and come together with right sides facing. The two of them have had their schisms and issues but are best friends to this day. When my kid brother, Darius, was thinking of marriage he said Erica would be his "best mate," or I guess the "best woman."

Through high school I was pretty much a

loner wrapped up in my studies. I did take some time to do some fun things every once in a while. I took enjoyment in writing songs, plays, and creating a Black History Month program to entertain the student body.

The school was a new magnet school so we didn't have a mascot and many of the basic things and celebrations most schools had. Any programs we wanted we had to create or establish. When I realized the first two years of my high school years we didn't have any assembles for any cultural events, I wanted to help fill the gaps.

In the 11th grade I remember suggesting a Black History Month program that was approved by the principle. I co-hosted the program for that year and the year to follow. The first year was an experiment and a great excuse to play music, dance, do a play, and entertain while injecting historical information.

I have to say the students remembered the presentations and a whiff of high school fame reached my ears. I performed a song that I wrote and produce that was buzzing around school. Students would hum it in the hallways as they passed by me, and tell me they "liked it." My school was ideal for supporting great ideas and the students.

Dr. Black, our awesome principle passed away from breast cancer and Mrs. Cage was our cancer survivor. Mrs. Cage never allowed us to have an excuse to fail. Mr. Flanagan known for his love for Star Wars and teaching outside of the box left a mark. English became fun to me and because of his out of the box teaching style, I fell in love with law and debate. Mrs. Brown helped me see there is power in my words and Mr. Brown told me to never give up on my desire to sing.

Mrs. Baylor forced me to give A+ effort in biology, because I hated the "B" I earned. She said I didn't give it my all and until I did, I wouldn't earn an "A." I earned that "A" by the second quarter. Mr. Smith made math fun and never stopped talking about the rattlers, FAMU. I thank all my teachers and teachers everywhere as they have impacted my life and the lives of their students.

The Black History program was so widely received by the students, more programs were created. Soon after, we added other culture events to the calendar to include celebrating Hispanic month in October and starting a cultural dance program. I participated in it all! Another reason I loved our school was because everyone had to have a 3.0 or higher.

Being smart was a requirement, it was cool and if you weren't an over achiever, the school would kick you out. So the normal high school drama I skipped, as did the entire student body. I enjoyed my high school years. Going to the dances was awesome because we all knew each other. There were a little over 100 students in my graduating class so we were on almost a first name basis. After going to all the dances for the past three years, I was honestly going to skip prom.

I know this was supposed to be a milestone in life and a big deal but for me it was just another dance. I didn't have a date for prom. I didn't spend a lot of money on my dress, and really I put the outfit together for a cheaper price than buying the ticket. I believe my prom outfit cost me $25 including the shoes. Against my first thought I went with my best friend Jazz, who also was dateless for the occasion. I thought we would look silly coming and sitting looking at folks at prom, but we had a blast.

We both enjoyed eating, laughing, talking, and dancing to the songs we knew—which weren't many. Jazz was a dedicated Christian and besides the Backstreet Boys, secondly NSYNC she didn't listen to much "secular music." So I made it through high school. I graduated in 2003 with Honors and a semester later I completed my Associates degree with Honors and I was happy. I walked in the spring of 2004. After graduation, I decided to fly the nest, giving life a shot on my own.

Alone...But Never Lonely

Alone at 18 was supposed to be the prime of my life. I had a degree. I graduated from High School without any born children. I made great grades, so I had several scholarships and grants. Yet, I was torn on if I should stay in Atlanta or reset my life in Florida by going to Florida State or Florida A & M University. At the time, I was passionate about video production, films, writing, and getting a law degree. I knew I couldn't do it all at once and so I had to make a decision.

I didn't leave Atlanta because my sister told me she might need me "real soon." I wanted my next move to be the right one and be able to help my sister if she needed me. I wasn't sure if she was going to move out with me and reset her life like I planned, or if she would hope for the best with her boyfriend.

As the date drew closer for when I planned to move out, she told me she had made up her mind and she wanted to move in with me. Without hesitation, I made arrangements to upgrade my one bedroom apartment to a two bedroom to accommodate her and my niece. I decided to stay in an apartment off the beaded path, perhaps the country by many, as that would offer a lot of time to be alone, think, and reset life.

I was able to get the apartment based on my theme park job and affording the rent was going to be super easy with my sister getting a job to help with the bills. We planned that I would watch my niece while she worked, then later go to school. I wanted to afford her the time she needed to set herself up before I went back to school. The plan seemed foolproof but after I moved into the apartment, I had to quit my job.

My safety became an issue, distance, and a slew of other reasons. So I had tremendous pressure to find another job that could float the bills before my savings ran out. I had saved up enough money to stay in the apartment for 2 to 3 months in case I lost my job. I owned my car because I bought it cash after working over the summer before starting my 12th grade year. I was prepared and with the help of my sister, we could make it together.

Although this was the plan, my sister struggled when she moved in with me. She got a waitress job in a nice area, but kept running into horrible tippers that made her question if she had made the right decision. Life was hard for her as she was accustomed to administration, clerical, and a professional atmosphere; having this job was an adjustment that was a ticking time bomb.

I thought finding a replacement job would have been simple, as I had a degree and experience. I was shocked, however, to discover my journey to finding employment was brutal. I had been searching for a job for over a month with no luck.

My savings was dwindling and I wasn't sure how I was going to make my rent in the coming months; my sister didn't make enough to cover it.

To sharpen the blow, when I got home one sunny day after searching, ready to watch my niece. She told me she needed to speak to me. She asked me how my search went and I said, "Not so good but it will change." She agreed and then told me she had quit her job and decided to move back. She said she hoped I wasn't mad at her. I quit my job, upgraded my apartment, moved out to the country, delayed school to help provide an escape for her, and now she's leaving me. I couldn't say anything for a moment. I wasn't mad, wasn't even surprised. Soon my words returned to me and sincerely I said, "I understand, in life you have to make hard decision that wont please everyone; but I trust that it will be well with you."

As she packed her items into my car and drove off, I sat there thinking, "What am I going to do?" I don't have a job. My savings is only enough to pay for the bills for the next month coming and then question mark. I gave up school, delayed my goals to help my sister and then I ended up loosing. I was alone, without any help, and my life needed a boost and I did not know where it was coming from.

The next morning, after my sister had driven my car back the night before, I set out to look for a job one last time. I had decided if my prayer didn't work—nothing changed but stayed the same; I was going to move into a shelter and give my 30 days notice to my complex. I also had a backup plan to live out of my car and the gambit; but as I sat there in that car meditating on my plan, I remembered to ask the Lord for help. I asked that He show me the way because I didn't see it. I felt all my options were gone. I had failed. Unknown to me at the time, The Lord heard my prayer and decided to do something.

That day going job searching was effortless and unlike any of the times before. The rejection didn't bother me. I jumped into my car smiling and didn't know where this burst of energy came from because prior to, I was borderline depressed. I went home and even though I didn't get a job that day, something changed—I changed. I decided the same prayers that got me this far, would be the same prayers that would continue to carry me. Although at one point I desired for someone or something to rescue me, I realized everything I needed I already had.

The Test

I got a message on my phone from my then stepdad that I needed to move back home or give him the car I paid for. He registered the car because I was under 18; he controlled the tag renewal, and co-signed my insurance

My heart sank and I felt like I was drowning under invisible waters. The two people whom I would have done anything for and had given up my life to help, now both seemed to desire to see me fail. I told my best friend Nina, as I had no one else to turn to. I didn't expect her to fix my problem, but I just needed someone to listen to me.

Nina and I met at the theme park too. We loved working in the Game Section at the theme park and vending was our thing. It was a peaceful park that could get hectic at certain times of the year. What I loved the most was that walking was a huge component to the job. I stayed in great shape working there. I started off as a cash handler and was soon promoted to on the job trainer. I kept this job prior to and throughout my senior year and on through my last semester for community college.

Nina and I clicked. She was fun and happy go lucky and so was I. I don't think we ever got into an argument until our playful debate one day

while watching football. We were debating about who was better looking, Tom Brady or Rodney Harrison. We both watched the Super Bowl with very little understanding of the importance, but were caught up in our game of rooting for our imaginary partner. We both cheered when they did something great and then talked about random topics during the "other stuff."
After my call to Nina, who looped her mother into the conversation, she told me to come over to her house and we would figure it out. I came to her house and told them what had happened including why I didn't want to return home. I shared how not having my car would end what little freedom I did have. I felt stuck—but knew there was a way out. I just didn't see it at the time.

Momma Analise, the name I gave for my best friend's mom, told me to drop the car off, cut my losses, and continue to move on. She said I should move in with them and come with them to Destin for the weekend. I took her advice; I parked my car, left the keys in it, and phoned my stepdad to tell him where to pick it up. I didn't move in but was ready to go to Destin. I trusted the Lord would carry me even though I couldn't and didn't see anything working.

The next day Momma Analise brought me to a Toyota dealership and said we are going to get you a car. I said Momma Analise, how am I going to get a car and I don't have a job, I have some money, but—she stopped me and said, "You worry too much meha." I stopped complaining and said a quick prayer and off to the dealership we went. My phone rang and on the other end I heard a lady say thank you for interviewing with us and we would like to offer you a job.

My mouth dropped and I couldn't believe it. How in the world do I get a call like this, right now? I told the lady thank you and said I was going to Destin and would be back next week and I could start. She told me to have a safe trip and she would see me when I got back.

I told Momma Analise and Nina what just happened and Momma Analise said, "See I told you meha," with her Mexican accent. We arrive at the dealership and I was super excited, whatever is going on, I don't want it to stop. So Momma Analise introduced me to her friend Iben, who was a car salesman. He was nice, welcoming, and helped me test-drive a few cars.

After looking and test-driving, my heart was set on getting a Toyota Corolla, gold. The fun part was test-driving the car; the scary part was the financing. So I filled out their application and the salesman asked me a lot of questions, I answered and he went to his director. They talked in a glass box for a few minutes and then he jogs over to me. "You have a degree right?" I replied, "Yes, I just graduated." "Can you prove it, do you have your degree?" "Yes." He jogged back into the glass box, talked a few more minutes and out he comes.

"Well, I am afraid to let you know, we got you financed." My eyes did a double take and I missed a lot of what he said but caught on to the fact I got the car. They had a program for new graduates that I qualified for as long as I could show them my degree. He said I could drive away with the car now but I had to bring back my degree and get it scanned in. I went and got the things they needed and I had a brand new car with 12 miles, paid $500 down, and an interest rate of 6%. I never had a credit card nor did I have established credit. I did not even need a co-signer.

I knew there was a God and He was smiling on me today! The next thing to do was to go to Destin!

Destin

The trip to Destin was so needed. Nina was Mexican and White. Her mother full Mexican and she loved the beach. I remember arriving at my friend's pool house. There was one simple rule, they were adamant on me speaking Spanish while in their household. I loved the challenge as I studied Spanish for two years in high school and again in college.

I drove my new car to Destin to help me soak in the day. As we made it into the city, my excitement was dwindling and fear was setting in. The drivers were so different from those in Atlanta. Nina suggested I hand the wheel over and after the person in front of me nearly made me wreck, I conceded.

Nina's cousin was appointed the job. I saw him whip through traffic. Dodge a Slurpee cup thrown out the window by a careless driver. While waiting at a red light, the car in front of us hopped the curb with two wheels on the street, the other two on the sidewalk and he turned right. I couldn't believe it and he said a lot of people from Miami are here this weekend. Any uneasiness I had about someone who I just met driving my new car, went out the window.

I enjoyed being at the beach. The calm

breeze, pretty sand, and gorgeous sky painted a picture that put all my cares to ease. Being around family was so needed and I loved my engrafted family. Family is not limited to who shares your blood, but extends to who shares your heart and cares for your wellbeing.

Between being in Destin and returning home the next week, I got offered and accepted two additional jobs. I was working three jobs, paying all my bills by myself, but unfortunately not getting much sleep. I had to switch gears because the time going by made me feel and realize I was not investing in me. I didn't want to work three jobs forever. I knew I had to sacrifice and find away to salvage my future. I prayed about it and shortly after I was sitting in front of a school admissions officer.

I had the opportunity to go to a technical school and get a technical certificate in TV production. This wasn't a bachelor's degree but was a great start and would allow me to see if I really loved production; and perhaps lead to one job that could manage my life.

There was a snag with my application and I was told I would have to pay for part of my tuition. The scholarships I earned had limitations for what percentage it would pay. After quitting one of my jobs to have the time to go to school and soon to quit another, I wouldn't be able to afford to pay my bills and school. I had a melt in the office and tears were falling and I couldn't stop. I wanted a better life and this school seemed like part of the answer.

The kind lady told me, "Don't cry I will

do everything I can to help." She called me back several days later to tell me she found the balance of my tuition and I would have a surplus of $500. I started school and was doing well, but I was falling asleep in class; working two jobs and school was not working for me.

I quit my second job, broke my lease, and paid the cancellation fee. I moved in with Nina and her family because I couldn't afford to live alone. By having my expenses cut down to a third, I could breath. I had time to go to school, to work, and spend with my family and friends. I was taking my sister and niece out for dinner every week to wherever they wanted to go. I felt free and loved it.

Nina and I spent a lot of time together and sitting around watching the Super Bowl was one of our down days. When New England won the Super Bowl we both talked smacked about who did better and the next day Rodney Harrison made the paper. Nina bought the paper for me as a joke. The cover read, "Rodney Harrison doing just fine with Katherine," after I made my modifications before posting it to the wall.

Something we talked about during the off-beat times of the game and mostly during halftime was Valentines Day. I remember Nina polishing her nails saying, "What's wrong with us? We are both good looking, great bodies, and with a good sense of humor—yet we are going to be single for Valentines Day. What's up with that?"

Replying, "It's not all that bad. You make

it seem like our lives are over because we are 19 and single. I am sure you can go get a date if you wanted to but you and I both know you're picky." Nina was a head cashier at the theme park and was working for a law firm; she had serious work ethic. Nina would not take any mess from anyone and if a man got on her nerves it was over before it began. We both knew why we were single, and it was by choice.

Nina and I had personalities that allowed us to get along with the opposite sex, have great conversations, and stay friends. When Valentines Day rolled around I forgot what day it was. It is easy for me to get caught up in projects as I completely submerge myself in what I am doing. I develop tunnel vision and nothing else matters until I am finished with what I started. So when she got home she brought two movies "Hitch" and "The Notebook."

We watched these two movies and saw relationships we both wanted to have, and we reflected on why perhaps we were single. Her younger brother Calvin also popped his head in the room to throw out a few jokes on why we were silly to fantasize over a false reality. We reasoned he was young and didn't know the facts of being grown. Calvin, I love you.

We laughed, joked, and made a pack to not be single next year and if we failed we would do this again. I love you punk! Nina and I wouldn't allow ourselves to be what we called mushy. So if we were to say something that seemed mushy, we

would through "punk" into the conversation. It got
us both through some rough times and always got
a laugh.

First Crack

Tapping into earlier, I had dates prior to my first real crack at true love and I am thankful for their kindness and time spent. They had characteristics that were eye catching but time, space, and destiny didn't walk us in the same direction. I believe every relationship can yield helpful information that impacts your future. It also helps build confidence to say "no" to the question, "Can I have your number?"

I had the opportunity of meeting a great guy who was a brother of a growing creative director in Georgia. He was kind, funny, and had I been single, I would have enjoyed his company. I was at the time dating a guy who had some serious insecurity issues. What I learned from him, just because a person undergoes a physical transformation, does not mean they go through an inner transformation.

This guy had an incredible story. He was extremely overweight in high school—I mean 200 or 300 pounds. He decided to get into the gym and he blasted the fat away, kept the 8 pack and was chiseled to the perfect football player bode. He looked fantastic, had a great smile, and we enjoyed quoting scenes from the Golden Child; I still giggle to this day thinking about it. "All I want is a chip," would have us rolling for a good 30 minutes.

He was a great guy, but I think he struggled—from his lips, with how I could like a guy like him and I was equally perplexed how he could like me. I was and am still such a dork. Nerdy many would say as you get to know me, with a strike of good humor and happy go lucky. I have been and perhaps will always be independent in that some days I may leave my phone at home. I like to enjoy my day and not feel chained to my cell phone.

Well one day I decided to do this and when I got to my phone, I noticed probably 12 missed calls within a one to two hour span. Now, if someone is not dying, in the hospital, or in the state of emergency, 12 times in that short of a time frame is too much. This was the last event that told me this guy and I wouldn't work but there were other signs.

A person who has already pictured you cheating or leaving them when you receive compliments from attractive people has issues. This thinking is usually expressed in an argument in no time flat. This is a personal problem and needs to be handled by the person struggling with the insecurity. Please don't try and appease a person like this, it will only cause you regret later.

Now about those 12 phone calls, 8 were accompanied by a message. The messages started off caviler, to agitated, frustrated, hurt, then to plan mad. The first message was "Hey give me a call when you can" and the second was similar with a little agitation.

The third call went totally left, and he asked, "What are you doing and why wont you just answer the phone?" The fourth, "Are you ever going to call me back or are you trying to tell me something?" The Fifth, "So this is how you do me?" and the six was "Are you out with your new boyfriend?"

The seventh was, "If you have found someone else you can just tell me and I will stop ringing your phone." The eight and final message, "Perhaps we don't need to be together and if that was how you felt you should have just told me."

Well, as I chatted with Richard, a man who adopted me as his spiritual daughter years prior, he said if there is ever a red flag for insecurities these messages wrote the complete word in capital letters. He suggested I put the man out of his misery and break up with him because his actions are unhealthy.

So I called him back and let him know, I kindly agreed that perhaps it was unhealthy for he and I to continue seeing each other. I trusted he would find the perfect woman for him and I was not it. Sure enough, several years later, I heard he married a wonderful woman and became a pastor. We are all human first, right?

Well, several months after that my director friend called me up and explained his brother was doing a talent show. He was looking for Christian artist and thought I could help him. I phoned him and told him I would find him at least one singer because I knew many. It's funny when you know artist.

They all tell you how their dream is to sing, dance, write, or whatever. You believe that they genuinely want to do this, so you keep and eye out for events for them. Then of course, you come across the ideal situation and you tell them about it. They are gun-ho and tell you they are going to do it.

You mark it off your to do list, and then a week or two weeks if you are lucky they call you and tell you something came up. So now I gave my word that I would bring him one singer, and three committed, but now I have none. I don't like letting people down and I know the work that goes into hosting an event and keeping people motivated. To help, I agreed to write a song, produce it— giggle, and sing it for his talent show.

Perhaps something worth noting, I used to sing when I was younger but I have lost some interest. I would rather be a writer than a singing talent any day. But for this event I will whip something together and give it a shot. Needless to say, I showed up to the rehearsal and realize this is the same guy that liked me almost a year ago. All I could think was the Lord works in mysterious ways.

The two of us hit it off pretty well at the rehearsal, but we were both professional and didn't bring up our first meeting. I admire people that can separate business and pleasure. You may meet the man or woman of your dreams at work, but please fight to stay focused long enough to close out your business before you try to embark on getting a date.

Your follow through or lack their of does play into the psyche on if you are datable. For people who don't follow through with their word in business, I cannot even think about a date. Your word, my word, means everything to me.

The following week, we pull off this showcase or talent show. There was no prize to be won, so perhaps showcase is a better title; but I did win a date with a seemingly incredible guy. In the end I felt like a winner. He invited me to lunch and honestly, it was one of the easiest dates I had up until meeting him. He was funny, kind, had strong values, and loved to laugh. His giggle is still contagious and his character makes you feel that the moment is bigger, more important, than whatever you are doing.

Third Date

On our third date, I was a stickler for driving my own car to dates, still am if I ever get out because there is safety in my own car. But on this date he insisted that he drives. It was a rainy day and so I really didn't feel like driving. I agreed and met up with him.

He drove this SUV that seemed perfect for him. Going over speed bumps in that car was like sitting in a busy boat rocking side to side. I understand now why they put handles near the doors of the car; at times you have to hold on and keep your neck firm so you don't rock it out of place. The rain is coming down; I had my hair freshly relaxed and flowing right. I was hesitant to get out of the car. I suggested that we did something that didn't require for us to get out in the rain; but he insisted, "I got you."

I said, "Alright, cool." After all, it's Georgia the weather could clear up any second or the sun could come out and the rain still comes down. We arrived at the movie theater and the rain has not slowed down one bit and if anything, it is coming down harder.

So before I could open my mouth to ask for the umbrella, he jumps his car over the curb and drives on the sidewalk. He lets me out right under the overhang for the movie sign and not one drop of rain hits my hair. He told me, "Go ahead and get out of the rain and tell me what you want to watch."

As I watched him back up off the sidewalk, shocked, impressed, and speechless, the security officer stops him and tells him not to do that in the future. I felt sorry for the other guys that tried to duplicate his kind gesture and got shot down. Their girls had to walk through the weather and I have to admit…I felt special. Before we left the theater at least three random guys gave him pound (a hand shake) and a few women cut him eyes that if I weren't present they would have left their dude to walk wherever he was going…and yet he was with me.

I honestly can't remember what we saw. I do remember walking back to the car and him telling me he liked me and I am the type of woman he was looking for "literally." Of course I passed it off and said of course I am; but he actually showed me his prayer journal, dated, and an entry was about the woman he desired to marry. The prayer described me to almost an exact science even to my height. But what made me think this guy is different was by our first kiss. It wasn't awkward, forced, or ill timed and I remember it like yesterday.

Our first kiss was a kiss on my forehead followed by a genuine hug. He made me think that all guys aren't full of insecurities. Some are capable of showing emotion and even smiling. He gave me hope that men can be romantic and perhaps life can be better than TV.

After just a week of knowing me, he was certain that he wanted to introduce me to his friends as his girlfriend. I had to ask him was he sure because I heard there was an unspoken rule about timeframe to becoming "official." When he made the announcement to his friends they seemed perplexed as to how quickly they felt he was moving. Perhaps it was because some of them were not ready for him to close the door on their chances? I am sure they wondered why her?

I guess the common saying would apply here, "Because I just had it like that." As a young woman I was a looker and my goal today is to get somewhere in that arena again. I have to admit, I am getting closer to the goal and by no means am I far off from my ideal built.

He and I worked on several projects together. We both desired to serve others and come up with ways to keep young adults having fun without getting into scenarios that would conflict with their beliefs. I remember one day I wanted to surprise him with a gift. I thought taking him on a boat ride around the lake, taking a walk Downtown, and then going to hear live music would be enjoyable for us.

He listened to R&B every once in a while, so I figured it would be a nice gift. We didn't get through one song before he said we had to leave. He felt we needed to leave because him listening to secular music in public could negatively affect his ministry.

I understood what he was saying, although I didn't share the same view. So we sat at a park benched and listened to the concert from outside that honestly wasn't all that bad; but it would have been nice to see a face for the tickets I bought. He and I grew close because we shared similar hobbies. We both were athletic, highly competitive, and neither one of us liked to lose.

Sometimes dating someone that is too similar to you can cause problems. It may be true you both are fighting each other to be the best, instead of learning to be great together. We both were writers, loved to talk and present. He was a speaker with a professional group and was—or still is a great presenter with much promise.

One of the earliest lessons I learned is never use the word delicious, to describe anything but food. Again, I am a dork. When I find words that I love to say I will use them as a common phrase to refer to just about anything similar to the Smurfs. I used the word delicious to mean cool, great, ok, and you are fantastic. Well, we were preparing for an event and one of the guys, who was a friend of both of ours, I said you are delicious and he over heard me.

He was livid with my use of the word, said it was "inappropriate and I am questioning your character" in his daddy voice. I didn't stop he's thoughts but encouraged him to question my character as I questioned his. If you don't know that I use words in unusually ways by now, perhaps you don't know me. He heard me use the word in many other scenarios and in fact we even came up with a word together that we used toward each other.

Instead of telling each other goodbye, we would say "bello" because it implied bye and hello together. Early in our relationship we didn't like to say goodbye. My grandmother sparked this interest, as she never says goodbye. She always said, "See you soon" or "Bye, bye, for now." She would never go to the airport to pick me up or drop me off as she said the emotions were overwhelming. I love her so and miss her tons; of course my Grandfather, Uncle, Aunt, and cousins as well.

I Want You Back!

Well this fiasco lasted less than 24 hours before we decided to squash our first argument after three months of courting. I realized now, you should never loose yourself to please someone else because you end up disappointing him or her and yourself. If I had caught this lesson then, instead of about 6 years later, perhaps we would have delayed our marriage, never got married, or got married and never divorced.

I remember having a conversation with his sweet aunt, who told me not to put my life on hold for her nephew or any man. I thought I listened but I didn't in hindsight. I remember we use to run around the lake to stay fit, to talk, and to enjoy each other's company. As we took a break to stand together on the dock and feel the breeze blow in our faces. We talked about our future and what that looked like together. We had a whimsical and perhaps unrealistic idea for how life would play out. We didn't know that war, family, finances, pressures of life would ever assist in deteriorating something so sweet.

After walking and trying to escape the night-time mosquitos that seemed to drill through our clothing, we decided to sit in the car and talk as we overlooked the lake. The bright lights beamed and lit the nighttime scene; it was so peaceful and chilly with the breeze. A part of that conversation that lingered was he wanted me to hold off on starting my company to establish a "nest egg." He wanted to get his masters while I worked to pay the bills; then we would flip and I could start my company while he worked.

But that left me with my dreams deferred. I remember thinking was I selfish to want to have my own company? To be set free from a 9-5 in search of creating my own 7-3 or 9 to 2. I felt I was young, no responsibilities beyond a phone bill, car note, and I had a roommate so life was simple. I believed now was the time for risk. I wouldn't have the guts if we got married, had a kid, and life began. I would be STUCK!

I remember sharing my fears with him and telling him my plans. He said they were cute and admirable but aren't that realistic. Then as we gazed across the lake in a moment of silence, out of nowhere there was a knock on the window that made us jump. He rolled his window down without thinking and it was security saying we couldn't sit in our car because it was too late.

We obliged and joked as we left saying, "He wanted to catch us in some action but that wasn't going down here." We both wanted to save ourselves for marriage. We feared overstepping that boundary would mean we killed the relationship before we gave it a chance to thrive.

He was a romantic man and although our relationship had very few arguments, there was one argument that stumped us. I can't remember what it was but we didn't talk for almost 72 hours. He wrote a poem, submitted it through the secretary at my then job, and that called me out of my cave. We made a pack to not go more than 24 hours with out closure. That was his favorite word that drove me insane later down the road.

Closure is a great thing but both parties' boundaries have to be respected. If both aren't respected, having closure is equivalent to one person having an understanding of their feelings and the other person railroad to participate. Hence, I hated closure because I felt I had to participate whether I liked to or not. If he didn't have closure no one got sleep.

I believe something's require you to sleep on it to be able to process all of the details—at least for me. It was not that I didn't genuinely desire to address a situation, but clarity on a circumstance may take more than 24 hours. So if your spouse, friend, or you want to sleep on something before you talk about it, I pray the receiving party would be patient and understanding to give you room to do that.

I could never prove to him I needed this time. It was not an intended jab to him, but a need for me. Perhaps if I had reflected then as I intended to in this book, I would have been bolder to admit our relationship had a few more problems his nice smile, funny jokes, and personality veiled. We had just made our 2-year anniversary and we went to a chocolate ball. That day I was wearing the dress he bought for me while in California on business. He was paving his way to being a highly sought after business advisor/coach. He was and still is a talented businessman with an eloquent speaking ability; I trust he will achieve all his goals some day including becoming a politician.

The dress was ruby red with Asian infused design made from a silk fabric that was smooth to the touch. I loved it and kept it in my wardrobe even until this day. He asked me if I wanted to dance, which I believed was a trick question be-cause he already knew the answer, "yes." He knew I was a dancer. I loved every kind of dance—ball-room, fox trout, the waltz, Latin dancing.

I remember several months back he wanted to take me dancing. Honestly, I was a more ad-vance dancer than he, so the instructor offered to have me help train the group. We danced with the seniors as we thought it would be an easy way to learn; but these folks had soul, rhythm, and a lot of energy to our surprise. Of course before I accepted the invitation I looked for his approval and after he gave me his blessing, we danced and I smiled and had a good old time.

Later on that night he told me he wanted me to smile like I did with no one but him. Secretly, he started taking dance lessons that he later invit-ed me to; and he was my only dance partner after that. To this day, I don't get out to dance at all and if I do I am usually dancing solo.

So as he escorted me out to the dance floor and we slow danced we joked about doing the

"Coca Cola." Salsa dancing was his favorite and the "Coca Cola" was his pride and joy move. He mastered the Salsa and could out dance me if I allowed him too. I had to take lessons to keep up with his footwork. He taught me several new dance moves, but my favorite was the "LA."

The Proposal

We continued to joke about how he couldn't dance a lick when I met him and now he could spin me in circles and I couldn't help but smile from ear to ear. Then the music was about to stop and he dropped to one knee and said, "Katherine, I love you and there is no other woman I want to spend the rest of my life with. If you accept my invitation, I promise to always keep you smiling and laughing with me. Katherine, will you marry me?"

As tears bubbled up behind my eyelids blurring my vision, I don't know if it was shock or I was mortified by the attention from everyone staring at us, but my answer was, "Yes." He got up off the floor and joked about my delay. Something to the tune, "I wasn't sure if you were going to say yes, you kind of kept me hanging." I buried my face in his shoulder as he escorted me off the dance floor. There was now a wedding to plan and I had no idea of how to do that. What was the next step? Then it hit him, we had to go to counseling.

I was down right terrified of marriage counseling. I am not too sure why I loathed going to counseling though? I guess I didn't want the counselor to say I had a problem or we were not fit for each other. I know tradition has it, women push their mates to go, but I was the opposite. I was surprised to find when I arrived at his school to pick him up—as requested by him, he said he wanted me to meet a friend. Soon, I realized his friend was a counselor that would continue to counsel us up until we transition to pre-marital counseling. There was a lot we didn't consider.

How our finances would work together? Where would we live and how many kids we wanted—if we wanted them? What were our families' expectations when we married? What traditions would we create and keep?

It was all so overwhelming and I tried to keep my head in the game. After about six weeks of counseling, I don't know if it helped or made us feel we weren't ready. We both got cold feet and then decided more was necessary as I had a rough childhood and so did he.

The dark, grey areas in our past showed up in our couples and singles counseling; my second counselor's advice was unfavorable for marriage at the time. She informed me our relationship seemed a little tilted in regards to him being controlling. I thought that could be, but on the other hand I never wanted to argue so I would agree to whatever he said. After two years of dating and handling problems like this, my second counselor told me to hold off on the marriage until I created healthy boundaries. She said I didn't have healthy habits.

She recommended this book on boundaries among other books. It was all a bit overwhelming and I spoke with my finance' and suggested perhaps we should wait until after his deployment before we marry. I put down the recommended book on sex in the context of marriage book because it was quite uncomfortable to read.

Our wedding seemed to be fast tracked by the deployment. He was set to leave for a year and I wasn't sure if he desired marriage or wanted me to be there when he got back. I never waiver that he "loved me," I was just concerned if he was "in love with me." In regards to his return, I always maintained faith he would be back but the war had changed him.

I didn't finish my personal counseling. I went to three sessions out of six and we decided to press on with marriage counseling now required— strongly encouraged by our church.   Yes, we went to three different counselors and the third counselor we saw every six months when he returned from over seas up until I filed for divorce. We never left counseling.

Sigh, advice, select a counselor that understands your background, culture, history, so that the advice would be suitable for your situation. Cultural differences can impact needed advice and perhaps it takes a person that can relate more than a person with a certificate to give the right advice. I appreciated all the advisors we met during our counseling and I believe without them we wouldn't have made it as far as we did. We both had parents who divorced so the examples just weren't there.

We made it through the third batch of counseling and I think there were some unanswered questions. We decided to live with the unknown because perhaps knowing everything was not realistic. Our wedding was set 30 days from when we started our third batch of counseling so we had 4 weeks to get through marital counseling, plan the wedding, and get married. In addition to these extras, he was moving out of his apartment in preparation for his tour and I worked full time while going to school.

I know, what were we thinking to set a wedding day 30 days away with all this going on? But that is what we did and we pulled it off. The wedding was put together and cost us a combined $2,500 or less. I know, how in the world did we pull that off? Like this: We decided to max our rings at no more than $500 dollars. I bought my wedding dress off Craigslist from a bride that was left at the alter. Perhaps in hindsight not the best choice of dress if the dress is supposed to bring any luck.

She was a sweet woman whose twin sister and her were supposed to get married at the same time. Her fiancé backed out and ironically I was marrying a twin. I bought my dress for $100, shoes, gloves, veil and tiara for $60, and the flowers I bought for $100. They were artificial and Shirley made the bouquet look fabulous. I almost took it back from the girl who caught it. Of course I got my nails done and beauty that was $60. I also purchased a three-tiered brownie with strawberries, chocolate, nuts, and whip topping for $45. I paid Shirley with a gift of $100 for planning the engagement and helping me to stay organized.

On the groom side, he bought the ring $500, rented his suit for $100, got the arch he wanted for $100, gifted the pastor $100, and had money left over to help where needed. We didn't have to buy any food or drinks because our families came together and took care of it. His dad threw down on the cooking—cooked very well.

There was nothing left over. Many of his friends sung and did some special number for the wedding. I came up with the play list, flyer, and invitations with the help of my oldest sister. My oldest sister put together my bachelorette party, which was a simple get together with close female friends at a local restaurant. We had a great time talking, eating, and opening gifts. No, I didn't go to a strip club, get drunk, or any of the Hollywood semantics.

The wedding day arrives after we are all super tired from organizing the building in large part the day before. Our friends, family, and church members helped to get the space ready for this celebration. I remember the night before he and I got into this big argument. I think both of our nerves were getting high strung and I started to doubt if this was what we should be doing?

This seemingly happy time was starting to loose the happiness days before the wedding. It became down right frustrating. I started to remember the warning signs my second counselor told me and was battling on what to do. I loved him, I believed he loved me, but were we rushing it?

My Big Day

It's the day of my wedding and all of the fun and happy celebration seems to escape me. I was moving in a zombie like state, waking up, brushing my teeth, and putting on something that matched. I planned to get everything in the car and drive to the church on time. I got to the church on time, aside from the revisit of the argument the day before ringing in my mind as I look at the hall; the hall was perfect. Yesterday ended with him being right and me feeling misunderstood.

I felt drained as I lay lifeless on the floor. I watched the time on the clock pass the seconds, then minutes. My older sister comes rushing into the room and says to me, "Katherine what are you doing? You should have been dressed. What are you going to do with your hair?" "Right, I honestly didn't think about it."

My sister goes into her bag and pulls out a curling iron. Shirley pulled out a body glitter tubed that she rubbed on my arms and legs. As my nieces helped me put my shoes on, my happiness returned. The people whom I loved, showed how much they loved me by literally picking me up off the floor and helping me get dressed.

I was happy, genuinely. I remember my co-ordinator said we couldn't get the wedding started until the long hand on the clock was going up, "you have 5 minutes." She said it was bad luck to marry with the long hand going down. Hindsight, nothing keeps a marriage together but the Lord and the people in it. Everything else is merely hopeful thinking and there is no harm in it.

Marriage is a choice that goes beyond a ceremony; it is intended to be life lasting. That was the goal but was it the mission? My eldest brother just arrived at the wedding without a suit, but his smile and presence was so welcomed. He had just got off the road from driving from Orlando to Atlanta and I was super happy he made it. I paid his wardrobe no mind.

So the music starts, the ceremony started, and it went according to the program. I did a great job with the music selection I must say. Standing at the door my father, the dad I had known for the past four years, replaced my brother on my arm.

He is dressed in all white, looking sharp, feeling proud, and grateful to be here. He never had a natural born child and I was the only engrafted daughter he had. He gave me a kiss on the cheek and dropped my veil across my face. He said, "Are you sure?" I replied, "yes." Our wedding coordinator says, "Are you ready?" I felt my dad wrap his hand around mine, I nodded, and the doors opened before us.

The room was gorgeous. People who I knew for several years were in the room—co-workers, friends, and family. I felt like a princess or something grand as I walked down this isle with everyone staring at me. Looking at the stage, I was impressed. My seven bridesmaids looked fabulous even my best friend dressed in an emerald green— my view a dark turquois dress. The dress was supposed to be sage green, but the mix-up didn't even bother me.

As I looked at my soon to be husband, dressed in an all white suit, gold vest, black onyx stud earrings, and a perfect smile, this day couldn't have been more ideal. He was smiling from ear to ear and yes a tear fell from his eye, which made me tear up before reaching the stage. While I saw his face and as I walked, I couldn't hear or see anything else. Then I stopped, my father lifted my veil and gave me a kiss. He put my hand in my soon to be husband's and took his seat. Looking into each other's eyes we stood there and he kept affirming me with his smile.

As we stood there and heard the pastor reciting the vows and the question "Do you agree?" We would answer with "I do." I tried my best to pay attention, and I was, but I was transfixed. I felt happy and yet the occasion seemed surreal. He looked to his Twin for the ring and as he slid it on my finger, he said, "I do." The pastor brought me to when he said, "Katherine" and as I looked up from my finger now sporting the other half of my ring it was sinking in, "I'm getting married."

The pastor continued to speak and my co-maid of honor Vickie, both of my sisters insisted on being my maid of honor, tapped me and whispered, "I forgot the ring in the room, use this for now." She gave me the ring off her finger and I took the ring and slipped it on his finger and recited, "I do." We were pronounced husband and wife and then we were presented to the on lookers. The pastor said, "You may now kiss your bride."

He drew close to me and I to him, then he kissed me with a kiss his grandmother said, "Let the girl breathe" that prompted us to release in laughter. The audience along with us continued to laugh as we walked off the stage and down the isle. As we walked with our hands one in the other, our guest threw rice gently in our direction. His brothers were not so gentle and instead wined up a handful of rice in their hands and beam it at his mouth and face. This continued the laughter and jovial atmosphere beyond the end of the green carpet.

Fairy Dust

As we re-entered the ballroom the smell of spaghetti, garlic bread, and special red sauce permeated the space. Laughter and music played on cue. We went table-to-table shaking hands, taking photos, and thanking everyone that came out to support us. It's amazing the appetite that develops in the bride and groom. We were starving.

We were escorted to the table set up for the bridal party, and we took our seats with food in front of us. My baby sis made the plates and my older sister helped serve the rest of the bridal party. I felt spoiled and the aroma of royalty returned. I guess the tiara on my head helped me feel a bit more like royalty as well. I managed to eat this plate of food and not spill one thing on this all white dress.

I was impressed as my luck is not always swell with making it through a celebration wearing white. The MC came on the mic and announced it's time for the first dance by the bride and groom. This was the song the groom insisted on selecting. As he led me away to the dance floor and the spotlight of attention refocused to us, I had to fight my urge to burry my head like an ostrich into his shoulder.

It was a lovely song although we both started joking about how long the song felt. We didn't complete the song before inviting everyone to join in. I danced with my mom's husband at the time, and my dad Richard.

As we danced, he kept telling me how proud of me he was and thankful that I allowed him to give me away. Several weeks prior he asked me if I wanted to meet and know my birth father? I told him if it were necessary for me to know him the good Lord would have made a way. He didn't, so I am okay with the dreams I have made up about him. I believe my dreams are probably better than the truth. When I was a child I tried to find him; at a time I really needed a dad and he never came.

I remember calling every William I could find that was born near the locations my mom said or had family members named the ones my mom mentioned. I called them all with hopes of finding him. Each person I called—that I paid my money to get access to, all answered the phone more or less the same way. Who is this? Why are you calling? How do you know me? Pause…No I am not your father.

I believe I may have found him then. He didn't desire to know me and perhaps his life had already started anew and I was an unnecessary interruption? Or, I was never a priority to be found after my mom made me disappear? I don't know the answer but I stopped caring to know some 15, 20 years ago. I don't blame him for his absence and I don't blame my mother for whisking me away for what she thought at the time was my best interest.

Not knowing my father did have a negative impli-
cation however.

The journey of finding him, the responses I
got, did give birth to lots of insecurities. Perhaps
perpetuated unhealthy relationships and I had
to kill off whatever it was to survive. My dad that
danced with me and shared in this occasion was all
the dad I wanted and felt I needed to know. I remember my dad kept telling me, "We should have
given him more time" as he planned to send us off
somewhere as a gift.

I am glad we didn't give it more time for his
sake. He died 14 months later from cancer. All the
things he experienced, walking me down the isle
and later greeting the only grandchild he would
come close to knowing, happened before he died.

He would joke often about how he wished he
could have known me when I was a child to experience changing a diaper. Seeing me walk for the
first time and say my first words. I am glad he had
the opportunity to walk me down the isle, see me
in the hospital after having my first child, and hold
her. He gave me powerful words of advice and wit-
nessed one of the first diaper changes for his only
grandchild!

I love and miss you Richard. His last words
to me, "Whether I walk this earth or I walk in
heaven, Jesus is always with me." Truly he had
perfect peace with life or death. I can't be mad
about The Lord's choice, although I was sad. But
the same grace that healed my heart, kept me from
completely falling apart at the funeral.

The first time I ever had someone really care about me—not family, do something for me without an expectation was Richard. He taught me so much about business, life, spirituality and my self. I remember the first time I experienced a mechanical car wash. My dad took me, paid for it, I was shocked and moved to tears for something seemingly small to him. We would talk for hours about life, experiences, and the Lord to the point his girlfriend started to get jealous and think sideways.

After meeting, her uneasiness subsided and we seemed to get along just fine. I think our relationship perplexed many as Richard was not my father, but he would stick up for me and disown anyone who challenged his decision to adopt me. The dad I searched for all those years ago came to me, and he didn't share the same blood as me, but the heart.

Without trying to crush my birth father, he showed me what a true father is and became that for me. There was nothing he wouldn't have given me and gave to see me succeed. The five years of knowing him and him being my father, was worth a lifetime of not knowing my birth father if that's the plan.

Right, cutting the cake was the next event. I didn't eat cake, never had a liking to cake even as a kid. So I got a three-layered brownie decked to the max with strawberries, marshmallows, fudge, and whip cream. The brownie cake was amazing and feeding each other was "delicious."
Had I known that would be the only piece of the

brownie I would have, I would have cut me a monster piece right then. My guest killed my cake; although I think it was my siblings who ate the largest parts. I wont mention names. I didn't get a piece of my own wedding cake and neither did my husband. There was none left over and I found it strange the bridal party said they didn't get any also. The brownie monster must have visited the party.

Lesson; make sure to have a mini cake you have for the bride and groom or save a tier for yourself. This is not the same recommendation to freeze a portion of your cake for memorabilia and to eat it a year later. I find that to be unsafe as pancake mix can kill, surely cake can too. This is not scientifically proven, just an opinion.

The toast was a bit strange after watching the video. The best man felt I stole his best friend and my oldest sister broke down because I got married first. I am sure there intentions were good because when the mic left their hands they both had more words to say. The event went by fast, our wedding, reception, and clean up was over within 4 hours. I loved my dress and I wanted to keep it on as long as I could, because theoretically I wouldn't wear it or another one again.

The groom had other plans. After the celebration ended, clean up began and was quickly completed. My new husband planned for me to change immediately so we could drop off the gifts and get on the road. He was a bit agitated and grumpy when he saw I was still wearing the dress many women wait a lifetime to wear and said, "Why do you still have that dress on? We gotta go and you..."

I was unaware of our plans after the wedding and felt it should have been no big deal if I wore the dress the whole day. But I didn't speak my mind, bottled my thoughts, hurt, and changed into something simple. I guess the magic was over and I wasn't ready for it to end. I helped put the bags and gifts from the guest into the car as he drove agitated to his uncle's house. We quickly unloaded the gifts there and got back into the car.

As we drove to some unknown place he pre-arranged, that truthfully should have been romantic, it wasn't ideal. He was frustrated because he was trying to get on the highway and to our hotel reservation on time. I was disappointed because my big day felt stifled. As we sat in the car, my gaze was out the window watching the trees, cars, and people pass by my window. The stale air in the car, the silence loomed, and I dare not correct it—I didn't know what to say. Finally, the music that was playing that I magically tuned out was lowered and he said, "Sorry for yelling at you."

As he continued to explain the frustrations he was experiencing I started to recall the warning signs my second counselor gave me. I wondered, it's not too late Katherine to stop this, we haven't consummated and if life is going to be like this, is this right—right for me, for us?

The reservations begin to creep up in my head and when he started to joke about the events at the wedding I paused. He talked about how happy he was and he reminded me of why he wanted to marry now instead of later. It forced me to push my fear, hesitation, out the window and we started this trip over. I guess there was some fairy dust just sprinkled into the air.

Not Too Late

So we arrive in Destin Florida and the weather was perfect, the hotel accommodations were nice. This trip was so needed; I needed a break from work and school. This trip became a vacation and a honeymoon wrapped into one. We were starving once we got there and thank goodness my sister packed us two to-go plates.

We had that for dinner and decided to go to the store after. Of course we needed something to drink, this hotel only carried two bottle waters in the fridge we didn't want. Something else we had to buy that had no use before, condoms.

We were such dorks and I think we were trying to determine if we were embarrassed to buy them. We documented the moment by taking photos with our phones at random places in the store to try to ease our nerves. We had an unspoken joke that we both understood and we kept the joke going all the way to the hotel.

I brought the book that our first counselor gave me to help me "mentally prepare for this night," as she said. We tried to read this book together and it wasn't helping. So we watched TV until we were tired then got ready for bed. I couldn't wear my traditional pajamas this night so I brought some of the things I got from my bridal shower.

I selected the one that was perhaps the most modest. As I exited the bathroom I heard a few verbals and I thought is this really going to happen? Crazy we have been together for 2 ½ years and fought these urges and now, I am not sure how to turn them on. So being the planner I am, I thought it best and perhaps romantic to put together a CD of songs to set the tone for the evening.

He came out of the bathroom and I realized I had no complaints with the mystery kept from me. This gift was one worth waiting for. The first song to play was Jesse Powel "You," and the others seemed too worldly for him. All the songs were R&B songs; I couldn't look at Gospel music the same way if any of them made it into the playlist. So we killed the music and killed the lights…

The next day it was time to checkout and before we left the city we wanted to go to the beach. We didn't sleep much and our ability to follow the GPS was not clicking; we missed it a few times. When we did arrive to the beach, the beach was clear, blue, cold, and the wind was super breezy. The sand felt hard under our feet. It felt like walking on seashells that were grinded down to pebbles with sharp edges. I put my shoes back on with quickness.

To look at the water was peaceful. It was a beautiful bright and sunny day—no clouds in sight. The breeze was a perfect match for the beating sun. The water looked warm and welcoming

to the sight. To get in it, however, was an ice challenge we were not interested in experiencing. We
left after a few and headed for home. Home was
the one bedroom apartment I had already signed
the lease for some months ago.

It was easier to stay there as he was leaving
for his first tour in the coming months and so he
had given up his apartment just a week earlier. It
was nice to wake up and be in our bed instead of
on a couch, his or my bed. Yes, it is possible to lay
in the same bed with the opposite sex and not have
sex—at least for us.

Now life begins. He leaves in two weeks for
a 14-day training. He'll return for a week then
leave again for three weeks. We celebrate Christmas then he was scheduled to leave before New
Years; but that changed to him leaving in January.
The next three months, October, November, and
December were busy and many of the days spent
apart. Life really didn't feel much different except
for the obvious changes, but my life was more the
same.

His clothes weren't there because he had a
storage unit. His car was with his uncle, so when
he left the only reminder I had that I was married
was the completed ring set on my finger. We talked
all the time and while we dated we became good
friends that helped the separation not be a complete shock. Plus, we were both active in our lives,
seeing each other once or a few times a week was
also the norm.

When the Music Ended

The first 14 day trip is completed and I leave for the airport to pick him up in what I think would be plenty of time. Atlanta traffic is so unpredictable and there was traffic. He had to wait about ten minutes, which lead to a mouthful after the hello I missed you kiss. I don't like to argue and perhaps as he says I avoid conversation to avoid confrontation; which by the way is not the same thing. Avoiding conversation is neither healthy nor practical.

Confrontations occur in all relationships. If there is a disagreement or misunderstanding, confrontations shouldn't scare you into submission. Avoiding confrontations can mean needed talks that address problems go unchecked. If unaddressed, one of the parties is sweeping problems under the rug. If problems are continually swept under the rug they pile up, eventually blow up, and the sender of the message may explode with complaints.

When he got home he spent a few hours at home and then left to hang with his brothers. We were planning for our first road trip to see a family member of his graduate. We were so proud of her. She had three children, went through Navy training, and left no excuse for why anyone cannot turn lemons to lemonade. Although the trip was intended to be great, it was full of disasters. The greatest of them all was we missed the graduation.

The graduation was to take place and we were to have solidified our plane tickets about two weeks prior. I was told the tickets were taken care of by my husband. I was scheduled to be back in time to make it to work, so there was no need to request time off. Getting ready for the trip was a breeze as it was intended to be two days, just there and back. I found out while waiting to board the plane we didn't have real tickets. The tickets were standby so we rushed to get to the airport and prayed to board the plane.

When I realized we couldn't board the plane because we didn't have real tickets, I was trying to keep my self from complaining; but I didn't understand. We had to be to this graduation the next day at 7am and there was no telling if we were going to board the plane. When you ride standby you cannot have any plans that have hard deadlines. Flying standby has no guarantees and it is highly likely you may miss a few flights, as we did, before you get to your destination. Lesson, if you have a timeline to keep, buy real tickets and sight see on standby.

So after being bumped off two flights we had to fly to Chicago because that was the only plane we could get on. We were told we could have a better chance of getting to Texas if we got there and caught a connector flight. We landed in Illinois and when we got there, there were no flights for us to travel together. Boarding separate planes was a bit frustrating and on top of that, we didn't land in the right city; we had to drive the rest of the way.

We didn't arrive to the base until after the graduation and the same day we were supposed to fly home. When getting on the plane with my then aunt in law, I tried to share my feelings on why I felt booking standby tickets was not wise. Thinking she would agree and understand, the opposite was true. I was unaware that it was her idea to book the standby tickets. I hurt her feelings, which was not my intention.

She of course told my then husband about the conversation and he scolded me for speaking my mind. I wondered if he would be this sour for the rest of the trip? To make matters worse, we couldn't fly home because we kept getting bumped off flights, so we had to drive over 20 hours to get to Georgia.

It was a long trip; but before we got into the van, rented by one of his family members, we went to the mall. Thank the Lord for this mini-van as we would have been stranded. At the mall he didn't walk by me, hold my hand, and barely talked to me. Houston was supposed to be the city of lights and for me it felt very dim.

After dinner, with a 20-hour road trip ahead of us, he apologized for blowing up and I became his pillow for the car ride. The drive was mostly pleasant. The largest grievance if I can complain was the music. I had not been a rap fan for years and listening to the radio for those some hours I almost went crazy.

I was surprised he didn't say anything as I brought him to a concert that had no cussing, made a CD with no cussing, and he rejected both! Yet, he sat in this van and said nothing. I guess you can't complain when people are bestowing mercy upon you. I looked forward to when my then husband would take the wheel and gain control over the radio. I had to wait ten hours for that but the time came and I couldn't sleep a wink.

Now the bad news, when he took over the steering wheel, he desired for me to stay up and talk to him. He didn't want to fall asleep at the wheel and I didn't want him to either. I had to be to work in less than 12 hours. I slept only 3 hours over the span of two days. I needed to sleep so badly. I desired to call in that day at work, but I had to complete projects that couldn't be pushed. So as we drove I was up being a helpful co-pilot. As the hours rolled down from 10 to 3, I was able to sleep two hours then drove the last hour home, showered, changed, and headed straight to work.

Walking into work was brutal and I had to suck it up to make it through the day. It was only by the grace of the Lord I survived the 8 hours and went home to sleep 10 hours. Sacrifice is a huge aspect of marriage; respect, and compassion is also closely related. After this trip, there would be another three-week trip. During his training I received tragic news from my grandparents in Michigan. My granny of 97 passed away and my heart was broken. I wanted him to be with me to help me process, but he wasn't able.

My grandmother and granddaddy cared for my grandma's mother since I can remember. She was an incredible part of the family; baking queen, loving, independent, and always sweet. I never heard her raise her voice to anyone, get mad, or even argue. She was a true lady. During her lifetime, she never broke a bone, and had only one child. She was self-sufficient with minor supervision later in life, even up to her passing.

As she got older some of the daily and weekly activities she enjoyed doing for some decades, she slowly was unable to do without supervision. My grandmother said on a few occasions she burned herself while cooking. Cooking her famous biscuits was a trade and skill my Aunt Monica took up and mastered. To this day, she takes orders during the holidays that prove my granny's special rolls still are a table favorite. Slowly, Granny was ushered out of the kitchen and the last element of cooking responsibility she could perform was brewing tea.

After she burned herself while making tea, my grandmother had to decided if it was time to remove granny from cooking and if it was safe for her to be home alone. To protect her, my grandmother put her in a temporary home after she injured herself. My grandmother was close to retiring so she planned on my Granny coming home after she retired. After my grandmother told my Granny she couldn't come home, she passed away later that week.

Bye-Bye Granny

The death of my granny impacted us all. My grandfather, aunt, uncle, cousins at the wake could not hold back the tears. The sweet old lady who educated me on the value of pearls lay in the casket. She looked lifelike with a set of pearl earrings that reminded me of a sweet memory. She said a lady should always have a pair of pearls in her wardrobe.

I remember one day it was storming and lighting. My Grandmother wanted to take a shower to wash her hair mostly. She told me, "If I get struck by lighting and die, you can have these." She picked up a pair of pearl earrings and told me they were the earrings Granny gave her.

My granny showed me how to be strong married but especially if alone. She never married, had one child—my grandmother. My granny gave her, her everything. In return, my grandmother gave her all she had and spared nothing in return. I love that my family believes in taking care of our elderly and understand there is wisdom and value in all people with breath. I didn't really reflect on the life lesson my Granny gave me while at the wake; but later I would have nothing but time to reflect.

When he returned from his training he men-

tioned the death of my Granny one time and I felt
he was insensitive to what I was going through. I
knew he was trying to prepare mentally for being
away for a year so I didn't want to burden him with
my problems. I did wish, however, he could have
been there for me. The time continued to dwindle
down as Christmas drew closer and his tour would
began.

There was an invisible tug-a-war happening
between him spending time with his family—who
would undoubtedly miss him also and I. There
weren't too many dinners we had alone.

We had several double dates, that didn't
bother me because I needed to maintain friend-
ships that could help pull me through the year
without him. The best thing about this tour was
that his best friend was going with him. I knew
that would bring him some comfort but his faith
in God would do the most good; or so I thought.
It was a stressful time where we tried to get a lot
done in a short period of time.

We managed to squeeze in another trip
to visit my grandparents in Michigan. After, we
planned to travel to Alabama to visit my grandma and grandpa Fisher, who were also not able to
attend our wedding. While driving from Michigan
to Alabama, the roads were icy and extremely dangerous. We got several warnings to be careful and
not speed. He assured my grandparents he knew
how to drive because he lived in New York for a
few years.

Flying in to Michigan from Georgia was

a breeze as I mastered chewing gum, and blowing through my ears to decrease the air pressure. When I was a kid and first took to the sky, I was in tears on the way up and down. We rented a car and he decided to show off and do donuts that made my heart stop several times in my chest.

Another trick he demonstrated was breaking so that the tires slid on the ice that covered the ground. I just kept praying we wouldn't be the idiot couple on the news that ran into a snow pile in the grocery parking lot. He came closer than I preferred to hit a snow mound; but he seemed thrilled with himself.

I guess you have to live a little, I just preferred not to be killed in the process. Then the Lord answered my prayers and had the car come too close to a curb that made him stop putting our lives at risk.

The trip from Michigan to Alabama appeared to be a safe and uneventful journey as we started out. The distance was several hours drive but nothing we haven't done before. So we set out early to arrive in Alabama in the early afternoon to prayerfully beat traffic.

Driving, we passed farms, lots of dead grass, and plenty of cement that seemed to twist on and on forever. The sun had not set so it was dark and quiet. I tried my best to stay up with him, but my eyes were attempting to close.

He joked and said, "Don't quit on me, I need you soldier," as we laughed our lives for a few seconds moved in slow motion and the burst of energy was much needed. As we glanced at each other for a frozen second and glanced back to the road, the light shined bright on a doe leaping past the car. In that second we knew we hit the deer. We saw into the eyes of the doe, and we knew the doe wouldn't clear the bumper.

So as the white light dimmed and our iris re-adjusted to our surroundings, we saw that the doe cleared the road. The doe didn't hesitate to run into the forest that welcomed it on the other side. Inside the car, it was dead silence and shock still rattled us.

The next 60 seconds felt much longer, was still, and we didn't say a word. The sound of the breeze hitting the windshield was such a better sound. Seeing the twisting road and the constant yellow path was such a better sight then either of us pictured. The silence was broken by us speaking at the same time asking, "Did you see that? Did your life just flash before your eyes like mine?" We were freaked out and could only think to pray and thank the Lord we didn't hit that deer.

There was no way we should have been able to avoid hitting that doe. If we weren't sure the hand of the Lord was active in our lives, we became convinced at that moment. We both stayed up the rest of the trip and laughed as we drove to stay awake.

We made it to my grandparent's house and she was happy to see us. She said she was shocked we made good time with the snow and holiday traffic. I told her how we had a close call with the doe.

She said, "Yeah you gotta be careful driving on those roads. Those deer just jump out of nowhere. I gotta funeral to go to on Saturday for a deacon at our church who hit a deer and lost control of his car." He died on impact when the car hit the deer and then the tree. The deer died too. The police gave the deer to the family, as was customary in this scenario.

A Hunting We Will Go!

During this time of year it was illegal to hunt deer, but if they died or were killed by accident they could be eaten. My grandfather loved going deer hunting when we were kids. He was also passionate about gardening. He would grow strawberries, grapes, blackberries, and other veggies every year around the house and on the fence.

I much preferred gardening to hunting. I remember walking into the garage to get a gardening tool one sunny day. I was totally shocked to see Bambie hanging from its legs with no skin. It almost made me vomit and I couldn't help but shed tears for the dead deer.

I have to admit, I didn't become a vegetarian after the sight, but I couldn't eat deer. Later in life I decided to pull back from eating a lot of meat, but the reasons were unrelated to this incident. It was a health choice, as I understand hunting for food is honorable, but for trophies is reckless. My grandfather explained to me the difference between hunting for food and sport. He said he didn't feel bad killing the deer because he provided food for his family.

I understood the reason, as my grandfather was a kind man; but I insisted I didn't want deer. He laughed and said, "I wont force you to eat deer, but you do know chickens are killed. Cows are killed for hamburgers…" I waited for him to finish as I nodded. It's just something different about killing and gutting an animal then buying one already prepped. That separation is preferred for me.

I have to admit my other grandfather, Granddaddy Lancaster was just as adventurous with food. When I visited my grandparents in Michigan as a kid, he would hunt for an alternative menu. My grandfather never made me try anything I didn't want to, but he would have you try something and tell you what you ate afterwards. I remembered trying turtle and squirrel that were both undesirable delicacies for me. I also learned the hard way to ask questions first before eating anything my grandfather prepared.

One day he decided to take me hunting with him. I wasn't scared I was "ok," or so I thought. Granddaddy insisted on me learning to shoot and felt target practice should have purpose. He selected the pellet gun he felt best for me and took me to the backyard. He told me to breath and look through the scope. He said when I was ready, take the shot and then we can correct.

We were in his backyard so I didn't figure we would see anything worth shooting to eat. Then out jumped from the woods, a hopping bunny, that my granddaddy called a hare. He said, "Alright now baby, keep your eye on the hare, when it hops again, shoot." I said, "Granddaddy, that's a bunny." He replied, "No this is food, alright baby SHOOT." "POW" was the gun as it jolted in my arms and released a fairly small pellet. "You got it!"

I stood there a bit stunned as the bunny fell over limp. My granddaddy jogged over and picked up the bunny by its ears, and I watched as his little body kept struggling to breath. The read dot on its body made it too difficult for its survival. As I followed my grandfather into the house, he bellowed to my grandmother my success. Then it hit me, oh my goodness I killed a rabbit. I couldn't hold back the tears.

My grandfather was so proud of me but my grandmother saw my face and said, "Dean, you nearly frightened her to death. I told you she was too young to be going out back shooting." I was terrified for a good ten minutes and had to fight to rationalize the killing of this rabbit. I had a pet bunny when I was growing up and I couldn't look at this wild hare as a hare; I saw it as a bunny.

When I was about 9 or 10, I asked my mom for a bunny. She told me, "No, I don't want no more mouths to feed." I loved pets and we had fish and guinea pigs at the time. I really wanted this bunny and so I prayed for it. I asked the Lord if He was real, to send me a bunny and I would acknowledge He was real; and it will prove He hears my prayers.

Later that week a young boy gave me that rabbit. He won it at a fair and the white and black bunny bounced all around the house. The bunny made me believe. And on top of that, the young boy who gave me the bunny was named Emmanuel. The name Emmanuel means God with us that I later learned.

One thing I remembered registering as I saw the bunny die, I am not eating this bunny. My grandfather made rabbit, turtle, and frog legs that day and later that week a squirrel. I appreciate that my grandfather is resourceful, but I could never drum up an appetite for what my grandmother at times referred to as "road kill." Chitterlings are another commodity I could never care to try.

My grandfather still hunts to this day and enjoys surprising us with his mystery meat every chance he gets. He is an excellent cook, makes the best breakfast (omelets are his specialty) and drinks—virgin and alcoholic. My first drink was when I turned 21, shortly after the wedding, with my newly affirmed husband and my grandparents.

He made me a purple drink, virgin grape soda special that was amazing. Then he topped off the night with an ice cream bourbon dessert that was fantastic. It was the drink my grandparents discovered on their honeymoon in Vegas some decades ago, called the Golden Cadillac. I slept well that night and woke up refreshed!

Memory Lane

So arriving to Grandma Fisher's house was surreal because this was the house I grew up in many years ago. The house seemed to age a lot on the outside and the city streets seemed to have done a one eighty in the opposite direction. When we were kids the neighborhood looked great, was welcoming, and all the houses were very well maintained.

That day, the city seemed like a dilapidated painting with vacant houses sprawled around the community. Houses that appeared neglected and in need of paint, masonry work, and basic updates like air and heat seemed to over populate the area.

I turned toward the inside of the house that instantly reminded me of my childhood. A simple time and place that in my teens I wanted so desperately to revisit. The house smelled like grandma's house and my favorite rocking chair that was granddaddy Fisher's chair still kept its place. This over stuffed, extremely comfortable gray chair that rocks and spins used to be the hottest commodity growing up.

This chair started arguments and crying fits when I was young. As we walked past the living room I imagined the furniture that used to be there. It was a white sofa set covered in plastic.

Needless to say, all children were off limits in the space. That plastic covered furniture now had been replaced with modern furniture that reminded me, times have changed.

As my Grandma brought us up the stairs for our sleeping quarters, I remembered we could never be up here as kids. With each step I took, the floorboards creaked, the air was freezing, and when she reached the top of the stairs, she opened a door we could never open as children. The glass circular knob that looked like a precious diamond opened to a room with a medal bed. I giggled when I walked into the room because at 21 I was finally able to go inside.

She told us we can use the bathroom upstairs but sometimes it doesn't act right and it is best to use the one downstairs. The house was a working progress and with my grandfather sick, she didn't have much help to make repairs. After putting up my stuff, I had to go to the bathroom and couldn't help looking down the clothes shoot that lead to the basement.

I remembered as kids we use to jump down the shoot and land inside of a basket under the opening. The basket was secured by one of us holding it, so no one falling into the basket splattered on the cement floor. The fun we had sliding down the shoot was scary cool. The scariest part to this trip had not yet been seen, and that was seeing my Grandpa Fisher fighting for his life.

My Grandpa was always known as a virtuous, funny, and jovial guy. Him lying in the hospital bed, tired, loosing weight was never how I wanted to remember my Grandpa. There was a nice nurse that came by at set times to help my grandmother, but she wasn't here today.

My Grandma never left the side of my Grandpa while he took terminally ill. She advised that I take this trip because she didn't know how long he had. I wanted to be sure to see him and speak to him if this was the end. Spending time sitting with my grandfather, laughing about the silly stuff I did as a kid, and hearing him say he loved me, was proud of me, brought tears to my eyes.

I know the grandchildren ideally outlive their grandparents, but I never pictured him leaving. Sitting in that room talking with him, helping my grandmother where I could, was one of the best moments in my life. Seeing how swollen his feet were and knowing the pain it took for him to eat, the work my Grandma did, showed me marital bliss. I prayed that the Lord would heal him and if it were His desire to take him home, that it would be peaceful and easy on my Grandma and us all.

My Grandma made the best breakfast my then husband claimed he had ever eaten. He ate at least three plates and said he wanted more but shouldn't. My Grandpa's appetite returned to him that day and he ate solid food for the first time in weeks.

My family members continued to come to the house to see me and meet my new husband. We got many blessings, happy wishes, and it was good to see them all. My Grandpa continued to get better as the months went on. He continued on solid foods for some months after.

My grandmother wanted to plan a trip with him because he seemed to have beat cancer. This honeycomb state of getting well had us convinced that perhaps it was not his time to go. Many months later, my Grandpa grew ill and it was a sharp decline. He passed away quickly and I believe with minimal pain.

When I spoke to him last face to face in his room, he said he would fight until the Lord took his strength. There were things he wanted to do and the Lord allowed the ones that were dear to him to take place before he passed. He was thrilled to speak to my mom before he passed.

I miss him and trust he is in heaven enjoying his needed rest. Rest in Peace Grandpa Fisher. The lesson, never hold back from apologizing if an apology is in line. Never delay to visit the people who matter the most to you because you never know when the end will come. Having peace when a person passes can only be accomplished if everyday you can communicate, love, share, speak, you do it.

When we returned home in early December the time was winding down and we both realized it. We were excited about being around each other but stressed about the oncoming separation. I remembered in August before the wedding, we took a marriage trip to Augusta GA. The views were amazing and the golf course was more beautiful than on TV. The sun seemed to beam perfectly, the breeze was soothing, and I didn't want to leave the hotel.

The convention was for only two days and the workshops took up much of the day. We didn't have much time to sight see beyond the hotel grounds, so we thought to return when time permitted in the future. The time never returned.

Our Parallel Universe

December marked our new beginning for how we both would live ideally for a year; that turned into the next three years—separated. Although my husband and I had only been married for three months, the time flew by. We spent about a month together if you added up all the days. In short, the first 90 days of our marriage, we mostly spent alone, although we knew we weren't lonely.

We both had great hopes and prayers for growing this relationship, but distance got the best of us. The separation created by the distance pushed us away from each other instead of bringing us closer together. We were living two different realities and we struggled to find a balance. Our parallel universe put a strain on the marriage that made the relationship doomed at the start.

In February I learned of a gift that was unwrapped, left under the tree. I opened the gift and shared the surprise with him. We found out that in a few months we should expect our first child. It was a surprise to me and surely for him too.

I wondered who would be there if anybody for me? The next thing I knew, I wanted my sister to come and stay with me to keep me company. She was kind to deal with the temperamental woman I became in those some months. I don't think she looked at me the same until years after, when she was pregnant with her son.

This baby was a blessing and I trusted God to make it stay that way. Although it was not an ideal situation I trusted God to make the best of it. I sent him pictures every week to document the changes and growth. I did consider that even though I tried to keep him involved, him not being here to see the process might make it hard for him to connect with the baby. This consideration became a fear that I overcame with prayer.

I couldn't imagine being him and he couldn't imagine being me. I saw that the one bedroom apartment I had worked for me, but didn't work with three adults and a baby. We needed more space. We needed even more space when we bought the crib, diapers, strollers, bottles, dishes, and clothes. Space was closing in around us and even the two-bedroom apartment we moved into seemed to be too small also.

It seemed like such a diva mode I was in now that I think about it. Here I am complaining about more bedrooms while he is fighting a war. He had a space big enough to only fit a bed and stand up cabinet to house his life for a year. I had my own bathroom, kitchen, TV, and peace of mind.

Sure, I had frustrations, I was fat, couldn't breath walking up steps, but food wasn't a problem, water, or phone and Internet connection. We were fighting to pull each other to see life our way; but our lives were nothing alike. When it was time for him to come home for his visit, the days

122

seemed to fly by.

It had to be hard for him to leave me skinny and come back and I have a watermelon under my shirt. I wasn't sure how to act around him, if I was still cute, I didn't know what to expect. I was nervous picking him up from the airport but happy to see him.

We saw each other and excitement instantly sunk in and we wanted to be around each other. But I noticed he wanted to leave and see his friends, family. For him, his normal was very much the condition of life before our marriage and I couldn't blame him. Marriage was for only 3 months before he left and most of that time was separated. He needed to find his normal and honestly I wasn't it.

It hurt that his time with us seemed out of place and I didn't know how to make him comfortable. What made matters worst, my pregnancy and school was drawing to a close and he wouldn't return from overseas before either completed. I tried to explain to him my uneasiness about the birth but it overwhelmed him. He missed the whole pregnancy and I couldn't expect him to sympathize with me. To understand the progression and my feelings about the delivery seemed another topic to discuss with God and my family.

So he was off and I was in my last semester before graduating and my last trimester. It was rough working 40 hours a week, full term, going to school, walking my dog, and keeping a house. I was super tired but I pressed on. So I finished my last class a week before Labor Day.

It was a joke that became reality on Labor Day weekend—I went into labor. I was in labor for over 12 hours before I could be admitted into the hospital. My contractions were crazy but my dilation was unmovable. My sisters came to check on me and found me on the floor; this was when they said it was time to go to the hospital. We went and I was 3 centimeters, you have to be 4 to be admitted.

I was put on a monitor and the ladies were confused as to why my contractions were so strong and yet nothing was moving along. I was there for 2 hours and nothing changed. She recommended I walk around and come back in two hours. So I walked outside of the hospital and came back, nothing, still the same. She recommended I do it again.

I am outside walking from 1am until 3am trying to progress my labor and my baby sister kept me company while my older sister took a nap in the hospital lobby. As we walked and prayed I said if I am not far enough after this, I want to go home. We walked a little longer and returned. It was then that I had made it to 4 centimeters.

I was admitted and no water broke with this child so that was the first step. The nurse broke my water and I went from 4 to 6 centimeters in 5 hours. I then opted for an epidural because I was up for over 24 hours coping with these insane intervals of pain and no sleep. I got to sleep on and off for hours. I did get stab twice and the first shot

I don't know where the drugs went, and the second worked so/so.

My pain dulled enough for me to get some sleep so I was content. The doctor came in and said I was moving too slow still. I was on pitocin to help increase dilation for hours but this baby was a slow mover. The doctor told me if she doesn't come out in the next few hours I would have to get a C-section.

It was then my mom and I prayed like never before. My mom told me to start pushing when I feel the contractions. So I did that. I went from 6 to 7 the next time the nurse checked and the doctor came in and said to me not to push. But at the time she told me all I needed to know, it was working.

I kept on pushing, kept on praying, and within an hour and half I was at 9.5 centimeters. The doctor told me "I know you have been pushing, good girl looks like we are ready." She got ready and 3 pushes later I had my baby girl birthed into this world. She was knocked out sleep and didn't say a peep. She was quite until they pricked her foot.

Before I was admitted I requested for my husband to make it back to the states, but they insisted I wait until I was admitted. By the time he landed, it was two days after she was born and I met him at the airport upon leaving the hospital. It was a loaded day and I am sure an out of body experience for him. Get married, go to war, come back to a pregnant wife, and come back again to a baby, then leave once more.

It was a roller coaster that seemed to not end. We needed help, so we went to the place we knew we could find some solitude…counseling. Counseling was a short-lived solution. Our relationship could not withstand the parallel universe we both created. I wanted him to be more carrying and attentive, but he had to be emotionless to focus.

He felt he was saving the family by the money he was making; I saw it as an escape for facing the family. We wanted the same things but weren't speaking the same language. He attempted to cope with life the best way he knew how and so did I. We were destroying each other and enjoyed life when we were separated than together.

The smiles, the laughter ended, and bitterness, distrust, and cheating seemed to loom in the balance. It was when I found several emails between him and a fellow soldier that I new the man I had loved and married had been forever changed. The man who argued with me over a light bill, refused to send the money I needed when I was out of work on maternity leave. The man that lied about his income he made for the past two years as a means he said, "to protect me," betrayed me.

I saw no need to continue in this parallel universe that honestly the cheating didn't matter, but wasting my life did. I wanted to do a lot with my life and until now, I put all those things on hold for the "nest egg." I had many excuses to leave my marriage but didn't get permission from God until the infidelity was proven.

I filed for divorce and the process was brutal and dragged out. I felt he lied to trap me, to hurt me, as he presumed I hurt him. I didn't want to hurt him; I just wanted to stop the bleeding. Fighting for custody was a hurtful battle. When I left, I left with less money than I came to the marriage with. I had 4,000 dollars to my name when I relocated.

He had the money he earned in his account, plus over 15,000 I knew about. I gave him the house and he gave me my car. I just wanted out and the only thing I cared about was the wellbeing of our daughter. I am sure that was his concern as well, but I get it. Bills don't pay themselves and hurt people—hurt people.

He felt he gave his life to save his family, his country, and in exchange he lost it all. The wife, the house, the child, the money, so was it all for not? I couldn't understand this before and I only empathized after living longer fully.

I too felt cheated by time. We created the best setup for our daughter and we were both alone because we didn't know how to walk together. We were young and hopeful to create a relationship that would last with no examples and time not on our side.

Today we realize we are not monsters, innocent victims, but we both participated in the life and death of our relationship as it were. The same is true; we are both responsible for the future and how we work together for her. We are both better parents and I dare say better people.

Reflection

In having time to reflect on my life thus far, there are several lessons I learned and would like to share. Being alone doesn't make you lonely and sometimes being alone is the best place to be. If you have to make a huge change in life, meditate and pray before you make a move.

Life changing decisions should not be made in haste, but planned out as best as possible. Consideration of how the choice will affect you and those whom you love must be at the forefront. Remember, when making your choices, you have to live with your choice first, and second, so does everyone else.

When I chose to get an apartment to house someone else, in hindsight, my sister didn't force me to get that unit. She was not signed on the lease with me. I signed the lease on my own. I learned if a person is not willing to walk with you—partner with you on a life's choices, they are not meeting you halfway.

To simply show up after the deal is done is not the best way to start something new. A relationship with no test that both parties have to raise to the challenge to overcome collectively, does not lay the foundation to make a future commitment that glues two together.

In dating, we tend to meet people and expect nothing from them. Then no expectation grows to lots of expectation for at least one as time progresses. What I had to realize long before I met my then husband, I had to be whole within my own person.

If I expected him or anyone to bail me out of my trouble, pay for my debts, fix my problems, I would be oblivious to the power that I had on my own. Not knowing your power can water down your worth. Don't let anyone or anything ever make you feel you have no choice. There is always a choice and you are always the decision maker.

Perception is everything. The way you view your problems affect the way you handle them. If you panic when trouble comes, you may sell your dreams or worst yourself for safety and security, which doesn't exist in things or people. True security can be found in understanding you. Your gifts, talents, and most importantly the Source of your strength make it possible to not survive trials but be triumphant.

When troubles get you down—first, troubles will come to us all. It is the world we live in no matter your social, economical, or marital status. At anytime in your life you have to be comfortable and honest with yourself.

You have to determine if at this time in your life you need to be alone, and if you do, do it. I remember when my best friend told me she needed to be alone and I didn't hear from her for 3 months. It hurt my heart, I missed her, but after,

she was stronger and our friendship was un-
changed. I am so proud of her.

You can analyze your situation and yes, even pray for the right direction. When we are around people, their opinions, information, fear and doubt can creep in. With every word we give audience, we can fade out the voice that tells us the right way and settle for a way.

I learned to not hate people when they let me down or even abandon me. Forgiving allows you to breathe and remove the hundred pound weight cast about your neck. Forgiveness sets you free. If you are bound, fear shapes and makes poor behavior or life decisions habitual. People are fallible and make mistakes that may not always be seen immediately. In time, however, the truth is always revealed.
It is vital that if someone hurts you, you let the person know how he or she has hurt you—in a loving way. No yelling, cursing, and trying to inflict pain in return because no one wins with that delivery. It is important that we talk through problems because closure is valuable. Closure, helps both parties to move on even if it is in different directions.

Lastly, I learned that rushing to your destination and missing out on the scenic route can lead to regret. If at times you are stuck sitting in traffic staring at a dull view, you think about how you could have taken different turns. When you have time to explore, take life patiently. When people are single, we can put too much time on dreaming about marriage, dating, and those special moments, we forget about living life in the meantime.

When I was single, dating, and exploring my new freedoms there were times I wanted what I saw in the movies. After watching "The Notebook," I felt real discontent with the people I had dated up until that point. Why didn't this kind, loving, thoughtful mystery man find me?

The next morning, I heard birds chirping outside my patio door. All my body parts moved according to my desire. I realized I didn't live in a perfect world, but I was grateful to be in the world.

I believed the good Lord had a plan for my life and some day I would have everything I dreamed of. I realized life would go on no matter how I felt. What I had or didn't have; who I was with or desired to be with didn't matter, because I had the ability to stop and smell the roses. Don't waste your breath and chase the moments that take your breath away.

The Grass You're On

While you are alone, you have no one to answer to and time seems to stand still when you sit on the porch and gaze out. Similarly, if you are a jogger or runner, nothing makes you feel more alive than that alone time. It is also possible for the married or single parent to envy the single, because alone time is scarce. Children are a blessing and so is marriage, but both require time, energy, and sacrifice. Having a family requires redirecting some of your time to other people that may mean delaying your dreams or goals for the betterment of the family.

For many this sacrifice may not be difficult in the beginning. As time progresses, however, you look back on your life and wish to turn back the hands of time and can't. Remember to reflect on the times that have made and make you happy. You don't want a temporary decision, feeling, to end a life long union.

Those that are single may likewise see those that are married, getting married, or have children and envy them. They see this life as successful because it is where they want to be now, soon, or at some point. The time will come and I recommend setting yourself up to be ready when it does. To want children is not a bad idea, but children require resources, information, influence, time, food, shelter, transportation, and a slew of other things. Get those things in order so that having children can be a clear blessing and not a struggle that may make you regret, hate, or even give up on your children.

Desiring marriage is a beautiful thing. I once described marriage as the living room at your grandma's house. It's the room that looks perfect, nothing is out of place, and only the special people can enter. I realize the best people that enter are the best prepared. If there are things you want to do in life, do them.

If you want to go to college, go and get an education. If you want to start a business, start a business! Some find it easier to take the risk without a spouse and children; others want family for support. If you want to do these things with a family, be sure to select the right spouse that is willing to support your vision.

If you want to travel and backpack across the country, do not marry a homebody unwilling to travel. It may be that opposites attract, but they could be the same reason that you repeal apart. Picking the right spouse requires you to know yourself. Many people pick wrong or allow the wrong people in their lives because they don't know enough about themselves.

You have to be honest with yourself about your dreams and your desires. I have seen many people in life that move relationship to relationship; as if being alone is a plague. Unfortunately, many of their relationships end because the same problem continues to resurface again and again. Don't be afraid to be alone to get to know yourself and hence better yourself.

Ideally, before stepping into marriage, there is some alone time that is needed and perhaps personal counseling before couples. Two whole people make a great marriage. They can speak to each other. They respect each other's differences—strengths and gifts.

Two broken people tend to expect the other person to make them whole and put a ton of strain on the marriage. As well as redefine it to be a patient doctor arrangement, parent to child, or even make the other person your god or object of worship. When we put unrealistic expectations on people or on marriage, we can redefine the union and make it into something it was not intended to become. Marriage is only as strong as the two people in it. It requires joint effort to work properly and never die. A good marriage never works with only one willing participant.

If you are married and find yourself in regret, look at ways for how the two can work together to bring about joint achievement. If your goal is to be a business owner and your spouse wants to be a C level executive. Then you two can select a business that you both may have an interest and work together for joint success. Often times in marriage we are together with someone, but aren't building with that special person. Teamwork and building together can bring you closer in a relationship and make powerful couples.

It is never over until it is over, which requires a person to quit. One of the best lessons I learned later in life was the importance of not being a quitter. There is a difference, however, in quitting and ceasing to continue in error.

If a relationship hurts you, physically drains you, is beyond repair, prayer sends you in the other direction, don't be afraid to activate the deal breaker. But do not quit every time the going gets tough because as you grow old and look at your life, your life will look like a broken maze.

The maze will have lines that went, bent, turned, stopped, and then started over—numerous times. Progression is too hard to spot when we continuously quit and accomplishment is always far off. Give life your best shot and know when it maybe time for you to move on—because that is a part of your progression. Don't let fear, doubt, and anxiety choke out your progression, but allow the light to shine and lead you to still waters. Some times, that water is still because you stop moving and start listening.

I trust this story will shed some light, laughs, and encourage you to share your journey to help another. Remember, giving your testimony helps you just as much as it helps others. Your testimony reminds you, you are more than a conqueror.

About The Author

Growing up Dr. Krystal Lee, known as Author K. Lee has always been adventurous in writing, production, business and being a die-hard entrepreneur. She puts her heart into every project and operates in excellence because that is the standard. She completes every project as if unto Yeshua (aka Jesus) and so she regrets nothing.

K. Lee is a strong believer in prayer and believes the Truth sets anyone free. She is grateful that the Almighty has come into her life. He has removed her from a path of self-destruction then set her on a path to keep her heart, mind, and desire set on helping others. As a kid she wanted to be caviler, not wear her heart on her sleeves, and not cry when she saw others cry. This, however, was not the way the Lord made her.

The Lord called her to have a heart that cares for others. Sympathizes with the afflicted, seeks justice, and helps the needy. K. Lee is passionate about projects that build up people, removes oppression, pain, and delivers hope. Her ambitions as a child was to express her thoughts and those of the silent in music, dance, theater, but especially in writing.

Dr. Krystal Lee has written several books both fiction and non-fiction that she desires to publish during her lifetime. In addition to writing books, K. Lee is passionate about video and media production. She started writing music, then transition to screenplays and theater. K. Lee is a talented singer, actress that prefers to be behind the scenes; she loves to tell a good story.

In addition to her creative talents, she is an entrepreneur owning several businesses. She has established Krystal Lee Enterprises and developing many more. She is also partnered with TUG Outreach, a non-profit organization that helps youth and adults by creating programs and offering services to help the masses.

Dr. Krystal Lee is equally passionate about ministry as she is with commerce, entertainment, and writing. She enjoys teaching and speaking on subjects relative to her life experience and anointed ability. She is a ordained Chaplain with International accreditation and she is in training to walk in her calling of being an Apostle. She believes Adonia (The Lord) has a calling on her life to be a mouthpiece for the Lord to those she is sent; she is prepared to follow His voice and travel to where He sends her without the slightest hesitation. Most of her ministry is online and published on Instagram, Facebook, and KLEProductions.com

K. Lee hates religion, spreading faith through fear, and believes in the value of men no matter their current condition. No one is beyond the healing hand of YHWH if they want the help. Help can be offered but must always be accepted, which requires choice.

Yeshua (aka Jesus) is her Lord and savior and she looks forward to His coming. The days we live in reminds her, the second coming is growing near. She believes and is passionate about helping all that have an ear to hear, hear the Good News.

Connect with K. Lee:

AuthorKLee.com
Facebook.com/KLeeCoach
Instagram & Twitter: KLeeCoach
Facebook.com/KLEPub
The Lesson Program & Materials: KLETL.com

To purchase books and to learn more about KLE's
Publishing division, please visit www.klepub.com

To learn more about Krystal Lee Enterprises'
projects, programs, events, and media please
visit KrystalLeeEnterprises.com

To reserve K. Lee to speak
Call 770-240-0089 Ext 4
Email: KrystalLeeEnterprises@Gmail.com
AuthorKLee@Gmail.com

Mail Request:
Attn: Krystal Lee P.O Box 1635 Conyers GA 30012

Order Books by K. Lee & Other Authors at KLEPub.com for special pricing. Need help with your Book, Script, or Play? We Publish, Ghostwrite, and Edit. Call 770-240-0089 Ext 1 to Learn More!

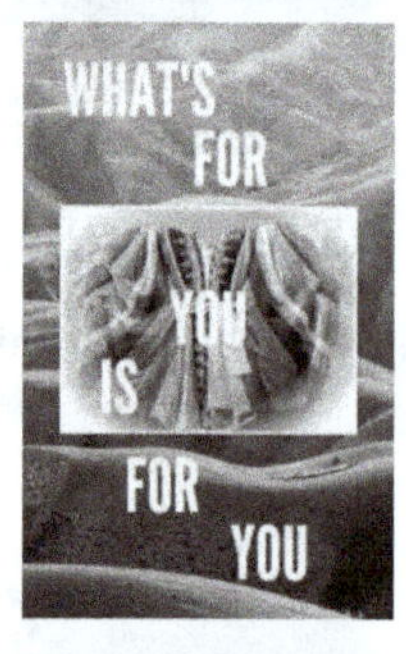

146

Order Books by K. Lee & Other Authors at KLEPub.com for special pricing. Need help with your Book, Script, or Play? We Publish, Ghostwrite, and Edit. Call 770-240-0089 Ext 1 to Learn More!